Comfy Monkey

By Kevin Dinwoodie

To Paul

Copyright © 2015 Kevin Dinwoodie

All rights reserved. All characters appearing in this work are fictitious. Any resemblance to real persons, living or dead, is purely coincidental

3.1

ISBN: 10-1512052442
ISBN: 13: 978-1512052442

Acknowledgments

A thank you to my friends in the police who do a job that I couldn't, to my friends within The Montpellier Writers' Group for their help and support, to Cheltenham's Best Book Club for their assistance and the biggest thank you to my readers.

One

Louise watched the parade of shops through the grime of the bus window and checked her watch again. She would be late once more. Her head fell against the cold of the window and she closed her eyes. The vibration of the bus pummelled her head and mingled with the residue of last night's alcohol. She snapped her head up and eyes open, perhaps she should have called in sick. She contemplated if Thursdays were such a good night to go out, town was busy, friends were out, but work was still due to be done hours after she went to bed. All night the weight of the impending Friday morning lumber to work weighed on her mind, but did not stop her having that "one for the road" or trying one last time to catch some guy's eye. She checked her watch again and gave herself an optimistic estimate of being ten minutes late. Judy, her boss, would take her aside and give her a talking to about that. Another great reason for not going to work. She would rush to minimise the time that she was overdue, but that just hastened towards the time when she would need to be contrite, offering more empty apologies to Judy; that ignorant, ugly, cow with no life. Louise was sure that Judy resented Louise's youth, beauty and vivacity and pulled her up for the slightest thing; such as being ten minutes late, or pulling the occasional sickie, or falling asleep at work. Lou realised her own stupidity and felt even worse.

Banking put money into her pocket and allowed her to travel, party, to live on her own (as long as she was frugal), but God it was dull. Perhaps if she liked it more she may have turned up on time. The bus heaved to the stop and she walked down the aisle of the bus, grabbing the vertical stanchions of the seats for support. Her arms were shooting out at right angles to her body, gripping the support and then passing the pole behind her and reaching out with the other arm for the next pole. She stepped down heavily onto the pavement and welcomed the fresh air, breathing deeply as if gulping in refreshment. She pushed on quickly towards the bank that was standing at the corner of the street. As she crossed the threshold she noticed a French man follow her into the bank.

Carl was particularly pleased with his plan to carry a copy of Le Monde with him that day. Part of the art of camouflage was distraction and his thinking was that by having such an odd item as a French newspaper it would focus people's minds and when asked "what did he look like?" he imagined a bemused and confused witness merely saying, (perhaps with a Gallic shrug), "French". And besides it was the only paper he had to hand. He had been standing across from the bank for thirty minutes, occasionally flicking through the pages of the paper but he took in little news. He was trying to stay focused on the bus stop, his own watch and the comings and goings at the bank. He was also trying to keep his breathing flat and even. Trying to relax. He was about to change his life, to take a step across an invisible, irrevocable, barrier and become a criminal. He wouldn't back out, the plan was drawn, now it was time for its execution.

Friday before a bank holiday would be special at most banks as it preceded three days of expenditure, special outings, extra food, more treats and more need for folding paper cash. In larger branches the staff would come in over the weekend to restock cashpoints as profligate customers plundered their accounts for more money to spend on their days off. This was a smaller branch; here they would just fully stock their cash machines. Additionally, most people would want to get away from work early and the security guards in the cash van were no different. They were ready at the door of the bank at opening time. Their well practiced drill was executed without flaw and they efficiently moved off on their rounds, hurrying to distribute their money and knock-off early. They had passed into the bank up to £250,000 of bank notes all in large denominations. Each single note had been checked and counted and wrapped with care. A paper sleeve carried the logo of the bank, the denomination of the bank notes and, in large numerals, the total amount wrapped within each sleeve. A colourful plastic wrapper sealed the expensive parcel keeping them pristine and ready for delivery to their loving owners.

Carl was pleased to see Louise was late. Right on time for him. The other staff had arrived promptly and the branch had opened with that unpleasant, grey old woman unlocking the doors. He had studied her a little. Her name badge was scratched and untidy. He suspected she had regularly wiped it and the gold leaf covering had polished away and the black, cheap, plastic beneath was showing through. He thought she would have been pleased to have received that badge some years ago. Her pride in that object was misplaced as the more she wore it, and cared for it the shabbier and down-at-heel it became. Her drab uniform had gone the other way starting as black it had now become grey and worn. Carl perceived her inability to look at her own unhappy appearance and to see that it shouted mediocrity as a serious character flaw. Why did she not ask for a new badge and buy new clothes?

And he knew she was hard on the junior staff, resenting their golden hellos and their new golden badges. Carl would push the pistol that he had hanging in the holster under his arm into that old woman's face with relish. Carl reflected and disliked that feeling, disliked himself and pushed the thought away.

Louise being late was usual and crucial. The bank was open for business, the cash van had already delivered and Lou would walk through the front door of the bank rather than ring and wait at the rear. Perhaps she would also be rushing and be less cautious than she should. She rushed from the bus stop towards the bank entrance leaving her trailing hand on the heavy glass door as she passed over the bristle mat inset into the floor, so that the French customer could follow her.

'Morning. Sorry I'm a bit late' she said with all the conviction of a kleptomaniac caught with a hand in the pick and mix.

'We have been open for ten minutes Miss Byrd' spat Judy from behind the glass of *Position One*.

'Sorry, the bus was late', lied Louise. She reached out for the keypad high on the door jamb and started pushing numbers. Banking did teach you the talent of punching numbers quickly. The bank was small. Too small to make into a wine bar. The sort that a manager would love to have under their control as bugger all happened and you had few staff to manage. Mr Major had managed here for fifteen years and would do six and a half more then go to Bognor to retire. But the bank was close to Cheltenham's town centre, it had two cashpoints that were well used and some good commercial clients. It needed a refurbishment badly, but he was not going to rock the boat and demand redecoration; somebody might then get out the slide rule and his cosy corner of quiet banking could disappear and become flats and then where would he go? To the main branch and have a sales target. Heaven forbid. Keep quiet, keep everything balanced and wait for Bognor.

The banking floor was dark as the windows held advertisement placards and the windows themselves had coloured glass inserts filtering out more light. The dark heavy wood counters that ran around the room and dark carpet added to the gloom. Bright lights did descend from the high Georgian ceiling but they were not switched on. Glass partitions framed the tellers' positions and only *Position One* was taken. The way Judy peered outwards, towards Carl reminding him of a ticket booth at the fair. She was not smiling and welcoming her first customer but appraising the man. He was tall, over six two, broad, short cropped hair, almost a military cut, he wore a suit, smart and new, dark, perhaps blue, with a faint pinstripe but without a tie, a bag was hanging from his shoulder and a paper was tucked under his arm. *Nice shiny shoes* she thought. She would have liked to have seen his face but he had walked into the bank then turned to his left and approached a leaflet stand. He seemed to be looking intently at the loan applications as his head was low. Perhaps he was short sighted. She hoped he was not going to ask her for large print leaflets. God only knew where they were. The loan applicant put the newspaper into his bag and began to straighten up. His hands were at his head. He seemed to be putting on a hat.

*

The door to the tellers' area was in the far corner of the bank away from the customer entrance, but only a few steps away. Security was provided by an outer and inner door, only one of which could be opened at once. Between the doors there was a small vestibule. With the code punched Lou pulled the door and an angry buzz sounded. She quickly stepped in towards the inner door and she suddenly felt his presence behind her. It was that electric buzz of another person in your personal space and then she heard Judy scream.

Judy had puzzled at the need for a hat in late April. Especially inside a bank and then she watched in puzzlement as the loan applicant turned and continued to pull the hat down over his eyes. It dawned on her that it was a balaclava and then that it was a mask. She remained bemused though her mouth dropped open as she watched the man stride quickly towards Louise whilst pulling a gun from under his arm. He put his left hand on the edge of the closing door and thrust the gun towards Louise as she disappeared from Judy's view. For a lady in banking used to counting coins, it took a long time for the penny to drop. He was a robber and they were being robbed. She screamed.

A sharp shove hit Louise and propelled her forward. She tried to turn but the bulk of a man was close behind her. She brought up both of her hands towards her face and she heard the outer door slam hard behind them both and silence the buzzer. It was dark in the vestibule but light diffused through a wired window within the door. It was quiet; her sharp breathing was clearly audible above muffled screams from Judy. Lou had been rushing from the bus and now a dump of adrenalin had caused her brain to call on her lungs for a good store of oxygen. Having another human so close, so suddenly was strange. He smelt showered and clean with a mixture of smells, soap, deodorant but possibly not aftershave. Her perfume was also present, sweet and light and it mixed well with the gentle forest smell of the wooden box that they were within. She was bemused, confused and dazed and gave little initial resistance as he pushed behind her, manhandled her in front of himself; putting his left arm over her left shoulder, put his bicep under her chin and his left hand on her right shoulder. As she was put into a neck lock she reacted grasping his forearm with both of her hands. His was a sudden, swift, aggressive movement and her only reaction was to grab his arm and take a sharp intake of breath.

He was tall, she was short at five foot seven and she pulled down on his arm to relieve pressure on her throat. She found his grip was not firm and she pulled his hand down towards her right breast. As his hand touched that area he closed his arm around her throat almost lifting her from the ground. She arched in response and struggled. The gun appeared over her right shoulder and into her line of vision. She had not seen it previously and fixed her eyes on it. The last real gun she had seen was during a holiday in America. But that one was police issue and holstered.

Carl said 'open the inner door.' The instruction, for that is what it was, was unambiguous, firm and authoritative. Lou had no reason or compunction to disagree. She did not want to stay in that box with this man. She wanted to get out and she started punching numbers on the door lock and Judy screamed louder as Louise twisted the latch and she felt herself be lifted bodily into the back office of the bank.

They moved as one as Carl lifted Louise by the throat and she grasped his arm. They moved towards Judy, the pistol pointed directly at her and indicating the direction of travel. Judy saw them close on her and she cowered back, her mouth wide open struggling for breath, she dropped her hands from her face but struggled to know where to put them she touched her chest and patted the desk, her screams subsided as Carl approached.

'Get on the floor. Under your desk!' Judy fell from her stool onto her knees and withdrew under the counter. 'If I hear an alarm you die!' As he said that he shot out a kick at Judy so that they all knew who his threat was aimed at. The kick was to her shoulder and pushed her further beneath the desk. She hit the paper bin and it tumbled out and rolled a little way, discharging its contents in an arc of litter.

'Mr Major!' Carl swung the gun away from the cowering Judy. Mr Major gulped and moved his mouth like a mute puppet, his little mind emptied of any useful reaction to his name being called. The gun pointed towards him, then lifted up and slightly to the right then a shot rang out. It was surprisingly loud within the enclosed space. Smoke erupted from the spent cartridge, cordite and powder fumes spread out from the muzzle and the acrid smell began to permeate the room. Everyone bar one person yelped. Louise twisted away from both the gun and the noise but his grip sharply tightened against her movements and pulled her roughly back to him. Mr Major had disappeared from view and was now as flat on the floor as lino, whimpering as dust and plaster fell around him.

'Mr Major, I want your money and quickly. This is not a fake gun. Real bullets, real hole in your ceiling and I would happily put a bullet in you *if* I think you are not doing what I want!' He strode across the bank, still dragging Louise and passed the various desks that filled the tellers' area. Most were used by visiting corporate advisors and were empty, some had computers and files upon them and Major was behind such a desk. Carl kicked him in the thigh to get his attention and Mr Major rolled onto his back and he lifted his hands as if to shield his eyes from a bright sun. Carl shrugged the strap of the bag over his right shoulder which then dropped onto the bank manager's chest. The bag was a folded lightweight fabric and dark in colour matching Carl's suit.

'Fill that now. No notes less than £20 and quickly' and he delivered another kick to inject urgency into Major as he rolled onto his knees and headed for the open vault door.

Carl backed towards the far wall and relaxed his grip on Louise as she was clawing his arm and fighting for breath. He swung the gun around the room slowly. Judy was not to be seen, she was still beneath her desk. Mr Major stood close to the strong room taking packets of notes from a trolley and pushing them into the bag. The two remaining staff members were as young as Louise. James was also on the graduate programme, he was studious, dull, spotty and suited to banking. He was transfixed with fear and had not moved from his desk since seeing the gun. He had only swivelled on his seat. He was wide-eyed, quiet and was not going to do anything to annoy the gunman. Jasmine was Louise's friend and was stood at the far corner of the bank. She had backed away from Carl as far as she could within the confines of the room. She was scared for her friend but calm. Carl was careful not to point the gun at Jasmine or James. Silent seconds ticked by, Louise made gagging, choking, gasps while Carl took a moment to steady his breathing and scanned the room, his eyes lingering on the progress

Mr major was making.

'Enough Mr Major, zip the bag up tightly and place it here.' At the words "here" he hit the gun on the surface of a desk between Mr Major and himself. It made a sharp, alarming, booming noise, laminate flaked off where the muzzle hit the surface.

'Judy' called out Carl. 'Judy, are you there?' A quiet voice said 'Yes.' Mr Major placed the holdall onto the desk as if its handles were on fire and then he backed away with his hands in the air. Carl thought that Major had watched too many movies, but hey, he did have a gun pointed at him. The gunman shrugged the strap over his free shoulder and he pushed forward towards the middle of the room and asked again for Judy.

'Are you still under your desk?' She turned her face from the floor and looked upwards towards him. 'You look like an old dog in a kennel. Bark like a dog, like a bitch, do you understand me?' She didn't do anything, she had her hands on her ears, but from the puzzled and scared look they all knew that she had heard the instruction. 'Didn't you hear me! He made a sudden darting move towards Judy and the furious jolt nearly pulled Louise from her feet. The move was lead by the gun that still pointed at the old woman's anguished face. His voice was now a scream that echoed. 'Bark you bitch, louder, bark!' Judy's inaction was answered by a gunshot. A wooden cupboard beside her splinted and the violent noise and disintegrated cupboard pushed her further into the confines beneath *Position One*.

He listened for a second or two and then he started to retreat and used his rear to push against the fire handle on the back door of the bank. The door opened and the bank's alarm split the air and drowned out the sound of a woman in her mid-fifties, cowering under a desk, in a spreading pool of her own urine and excrement, pretending to bark like a dog, whilst sobbing.

Two

Grace Taylor swung out of bed as the phone rang. She had had a long shift the night before as she wanted to ensure that the debrief, processing and paperwork was completed before she clocked off. She didn't work late for the overtime, that wasn't an option for her rank, she just wanted to do the job properly, to a standard that no one could question. It was her sergeant on the phone, he didn't need any introduction.

'Ma'am, we are getting reports of an armed robbery.'

'Where?'

'Ambrose Street, close to you and it is going on now.' There was an absence of urgency in his voice.

'Can you send a car for me?'

'It's on the way already.'

She hung up whilst walking to the bathroom and put the phone down next to the toothpaste and picked that up with the brush. She got into the shower whilst she brushed her teeth. Her father had taught her to brush teeth first before washing. It was a bacteria thing. Doing both simultaneously would be OK as well. She was wearing pants (another bacteria thing) but swept those off as she soaped herself and then climbed back out of the shower. She wanted to keep her hair short as it was more practical for days such as this, but she knew she looked better with longer hair. She just avoided getting it too wet and would wash it later.

She towelled herself as she walked back into the bedroom and pulled open her lingerie drawer and selected the best pants and bra for that day. Black, business like and not overtly sexy. She passed over the bright polka dots and the chintz for more sedate items. But she did select her more expensive brands as today was a day for some spirit and confidence. She thought her dad would approve, then realised that he would rather not think about his daughter's underwear. She pulled on a black polo neck top and black tights. A light grey skirt and matching jacket were selected next and then she stood by the front door applying moisturiser. A wide shelf held all the items she had shed the night before when she had entered the flat and she walked down the hallway towards the door picking up and selecting items as she went. Watch, an expensive but not too flashy one. Key fob without the car keys, just the house keys. She had good keys for some good locks as she liked the security and she had been to far too many burglaries that could have been saved by better locks. Police radio, big and bulky but charged and probably invaluable today. Wallet, with £180 cash and cards, she never liked to be short and she would get more today as £250 was a better number. Her mobile, retrieved from beside the toothpaste, was next. It was small and expensive. She used to have a solid, hardwearing, functional one but she had seen a builder with one similar and instantly went to the first phone shop she saw to buy something girly. The phone, wallet and keys went into the selected handbag, (several were available at the end of the shelf) and she stepped into the favoured shoes for the day. Good heels but less severe than those from the previous day. She opened the door and pulled a hair brush out of the bag and descended the stairs from her flat. She could see the patrol car through the frosted glass as she walked to the door. That was ten minutes from bed to door and she could tell from the look of the PC waiting by the car that she looked good. She had spent her time well. Pity about breakfast though.

Three

Carl twisted sharply as he backed through the rear door of the bank. Louise continued to be held against him by the neck lock. His right arm was held in front of him with the gun in his line of sight as his gaze swung through the alley at the back of the bank. He kicked the door closed. The alarm was muffled as they stood in the relative quiet of the small car park at the rear of the bank.

'I have no plans to harm you in any way', Carl said to Louise as he relaxed his grip. His mouth was in close proximity to her ear and he said those words softly. 'I do need your protection to help me get away from here.' He clicked the safety on the gun and relaxed his grip enough to holster it under his left armpit. For a second she considered bolting but his grip only relented momentarily and he propelled her along the wide alley behind the bank.

'Where are we going?' The first words she had said to him.

'We won't walk far, I do have transport' and with that he moved her left towards the garage of the business beside the bank. There, next to the overflowing bins was a motorbike. Louise was no stranger to motorbikes, she had always been a good looking girl from the poor side of town and she had spent time with a group of guys whose only mode of transport were motorbikes. She remembered the speed, freedom and thrill of riding pillion. The English weather had sometimes left her cold and another group of boys from the wealthy side of town, who could afford four wheels began to appeal. However, the thought of being on a bike with a gun toting robber was not as appealing as an easy-going teenage boy. She looked for an escape route. Carl was a step ahead of her and as he swung his right leg over the saddle he kept a tight grip on her left wrist with his left hand. He pushed the starter and blipped the throttle. The bag's strap was swung over his shoulder and head and the bag itself positioned over his thigh. He then pulled her hand closer to his left handle bar. There was a thin coil of wire attached to it and the free end was twisted into a snare. She flexed her knees in reaction and pushed back. He twisted her wrist and applied pressure to ensure she relented and placed the snare over her wrist and pulled it snug. He then reversed the twisting pressure on her wrist to make her move towards him and with a nodding head he motioned that she should get on to the pillion. She tried to stand firm. He raised his voice over the engine.

'Get on, I won't keep you long and I only need the wire to ensure that you don't jump off at the lights. If the bike and you go in different directions then it will hurt. Best you stay with me.' She could see no alternative now that the cheese-wire noose was over her wrist. She climbed on. Some slack wire coiled out and she could see that she was like a dog on a thin leash. In the distance she heard a police siren, but that was drowned as Carl stamped down into gear, revved and departed at speed. She instinctively grasped him around the waist and hung on.

They went the wrong way. Away from the road and towards a dead end. So dead that Louise had never ventured down it. The cul-de-sac had a few cars parked in it and Carl deftly decelerated and picked his way through the cars and entered a short footpath leading onto another road. He lifted his head like a meerkat to look left and right to spot any traffic. On their left was a graveyard and he had a good view over the low memorials to know that nothing was approaching from that way. On the right was a chain-link fence, an office car park then a garden. This again afforded an open view of no traffic. Carl looked straight ahead at another road that stretched ahead of them and that was his direction of travel. Seeing that nothing was coming he opened the throttle to the stop. He left the alley way, crossed the pavement and left the ground for a metre as he went straight across the road junction. He lifted the gear lever with his toe, released the throttle an iota to allow the pressure to release on the drive train and applied full power again to affect a clutch-less change and then another before getting hard on the brakes as they approached a mini roundabout.

With a bag of money, no gloves, no helmets and a pillion wired to the dashboard some care must be taken with navigating the traffic. As he accelerated and decelerated she was forced fore and aft and the sudden speed and noise pressed into her skull. She feared for losing her grip, falling and then losing her hand so she buried her head between his shoulder blades. For a moment she closed her eyes and then had the foresight to examine where she was. She would need to keep her bearings.

They crossed the mini roundabout without any deviation from the straight ahead and entered a rough-ground car park. Carl barrelled across it and left via a pedestrian pathway onto the scenic footpath beside the river Chelt. He pitched the bike right and split the air with the wail of the engine and a plume of two stroke oil as he headed along the footpath. He swivelled at this point and looked over his shoulder towards Louise and put his left hand on her thigh and he shouted 'are you OK?' As dumb questions go, it was right up there, but she offered the auto reply of 'yes' into his back. The alleyway was approaching a junction with a main road and the throttle was released towards tick over as they slowed and emerged into the main road. A police car shot over a junction away to their left. It flashed by with a howl of sirens, lights and colour, like a glimpse of a fairground ride. They crossed the pavement, slewed across the road between some stationary traffic on their side, and moving traffic on the far side, and then they accelerated away along a back road that provided trade access to a hotel. That road emerged into a more genteel crescent in a quieter part of Cheltenham. The properties were larger here but still commercial. Companies had bought the villas and houses as prestigious offices and few individuals had the wherewithal to retain these large places as a private home. The trail bike sped along the wide avenue with Carl leaning the bike over as the speed increased on the crescent's steady camber. As the road emerged onto a wide tee junction Louise felt the urgency change, the speed decreased and as Carl lined the bike up with another alleyway the engine died and they freewheeled along the alley, listening to the squeak of a chain in need of oil and tyre rubber on tarmac. As the alley emerged into the closed end of a mews Carl stopped close to a wall.

'Off you get.' She swung her leg over the saddle and stepped down from the pillion peg. The intense vibration left her a little numb and her ears rang from the exhaust note. She moved to comb her hair into place and the wire pulled tight and she started. Carl had already pulled a small pair of pliers from the side pocket of his suit and snipped the wire. Whilst he freed her from the noose he grasped her wrist tightly. He stepped off the bike and left it leaning against the wall. He then changed hands so that he had her left wrist in his right hand and walked down the alley.

'I have a car here' he added and motioned towards a low archway, with a house built over it, that led to another road and one of Cheltenham's many parks. 'I still need your protection until I am out of town and then I will let you go and give you some of this to stash.' He nodded towards the holdall as he said the word "some of this". He pulled off the balaclava and put it into the holdall as they emerged from the gloom of the tunnel into the April sunshine. 'When we're in the car I will give you some cash and I'll let you go in half an hour.'

'I don't want any money' she said as they approached a modern, clean saloon car parked against the curb at the end of the alley.

'OK; well, it is a carrot or a stick approach at the moment and I think we would both prefer carrot' and with that he put his hand into his jacket. Louise froze expecting to see the gun emerge but Carl's hand appeared with some keys and the car's locks thunked open. He stood beside and behind her as he opened the passenger door and compelled her into the car. As the door closed she instinctively thought to lock him out. She scanned the interior door panel, she had no idea how to lock the door and the fact that there was an ugly scar in the otherwise pristine interior perplexed her. She realised that the lever to open the passenger door had been removed. The rear door opened and the holdall fell onto the rear seat and then swiftly the driver's door was open and Carl dropped into the car and once again Louise and he were in a confined space.

Four

Grace opened the patrol car door before it came to a halt and then stepped out onto the pavement and stood toe-to-toe with her sergeant and asked 'so, who did it?'

The solving of serious crimes in a small town is sometimes not very difficult. You could resolve car thefts by simply realising that car thieves who attend court and don't get sent down needed to get home again afterwards. But there were many car thieves. Acts, such as bank robbery, are not the transgressions of normal men. These are not the accident of circumstance or opportunity. Planning and thinking are required and often practice. Sergeant Harper had walked and driven and sat (and been flat on his back a few times) on this beat and knew the likely culprits of a bank robbery.

'No idea', he said. Grace did not disguise her disappointment and pulled a face of incredulity.

'No idea', she repeated and continued with a hopeful 'you mean that it was an outsider?' She meant someone from out of town.

'No, I do mean that I have no idea.' He made a movement with his head to show that he was still weighing things up. 'I just can't think who this one could belong to. Firstly they fired shots, live rounds. Nine millimetres. They left the shell casing. So someone with a gun and who is willing to let a round go. Most of the locals either don't have a real gun or would have issues with getting live rounds. This was someone ma'am who has access to firearms and shells.'

'So it is an outsider?' repeated Grace.

'Well, I don't believe so. We had a call reporting

a man acting suspiciously in Leckhampton ten minutes before this all took off.' Harper pointed his thumb over his shoulder to indicate he meant the robbery, 'and then five minutes before another call saying a man with a handgun was outside the Abbey National in Charlton Kings.'

'And so what little we had was on the way to opposite ends of town as this happened' added Grace.

'Now you don't need to be Einstein to do that but it shows some knowledge. But the getaway route is important. On a motorbike using alleys and back roads so another clue of a local. Did I say he took a hostage?'

Grace pulled another face showing some surprise. 'Who?'

'Louise Byrd, twenty-five, single, lives in Montpellier, worked at the bank eight months on a graduate-high-flyer entry thing.' Harper's intonation changed as he said "graduate-high-flyer entry thing", his head lowered and he shot his boss a look of apology. He might have just said the wrong thing. She, with much less service, experience and nouse than he, earned much more and had much better prospects due to a degree in criminology and a dad who had been Chief Constable. She turns to his knowledge to put a name to a crime and to assemble the prime suspects. But she takes the glory as she has the rank and a degree. Only five years to go before he retires and she will be off up the greasy pole way before then *if* she can solve a few more bank robberies. He could have hated her if she didn't have raw charisma and the work ethic to win him over.

'So, what local bank robbers do you know who fire guns, ride motorcycles and take hostages?' Grace asked Harper with some exasperation.

'Gareth Chambers and John Fellows ma'am.'

Another look of exasperation spread over Grace's face and she pursed her lips and nodded slowly.

'You got out of the wrong side of bed this morning didn't you. Chambers is dead and Fellows is five foot tall, with four foot long dreadlocks and a Glaswegian accent. You could say he stands out in a crowd. If it were him we would be outside his house. I don't need to be Morse to know that you are taking the piss.'

Grace was not a fan of older, predominantly male, colleagues taking consideration of her good looks, connections and privileges to assume that she could not think for herself. Harper was a good copper and did have an encyclopaedic knowledge of villains. But he could be a moody twat sometimes. Today she had assumed too much of him. Sometimes he could identify a burglar from an entry method at a hundred paces and she thought he would have known his man on this job. She could have hated him if he had not been so good at his job and the most caring man in her life, besides her father.

'OK' said Grace starting over, 'we have no idea who did this.' She emphasised the word "we".

<u>Five</u>

The description of the bike was circulated, higher authorities were advised of the hostage and the media were advised to get some more eyes looking for Louise and her kidnapper. Harper and Grace took a tour of the building, keeping away from the white clad Scenes of Crime team and the bank staff and then stood outside the rear door looking up at the building.

'So a lone gunman, just after the cash delivery and he arrived at the same time as Louise.'

'And she was late' added Harper.

'Inside involvement then?'

'Well, it's not the biggest branch of Lloyds, so he could have got more somewhere else, so he, or they, had a reason to take this branch.'

'But' said Grace to add some balance, 'the security here is crap as it is a small backwater branch.' She stood back and placed a hand on each hip and frowned as she swung too and fro looking up and down the road at the rear of the bank. 'He did seem to know his way around but he needed to get into the back of the branch and that is where Louise came in very handy. She let him through the security doors. I think we need to have a look at Miss Byrd. Can you arrange a search warrant for her place and let's have a chat to the staff.'

Harper and Grace had a standard interrogation technique. It was not pre-planned, it had evolved. They tended to alternate with the questions. One would pose a question. The other would probe deeper and then the other would either probe deeper still or repeat back to the subject what the two had just learnt. To an outsider listening-in you might also simply think they both just wanted to have the last word.

'So, you saw him enter the bank Miss Tate?' Harper began.

'Well yes, but I was looking at Louise, she was late again you see and so I did not really see him.'

'Did not *really* see him' replayed Grace. 'You did notice something though didn't you Judy, tell us your impression of him.'

'He was tall and big, with a short hair cut. Perhaps military!' exclaimed Judy as if all would now fall into place, the crime would be solved because she had spotted that the robber had been in the forces.

Harper asked 'did you think he was a soldier when you first saw him?' He paused and Judy looked blank. 'I ask that as he did have a gun and so you may now think he was military because of that. So it is important to know when you thought he was military.' More pause then Judy said 'When I first saw him.'

'Good' said Grace smiling at Judy. So he had a military appearance, that may be useful to us.

'Did you get on with Louise?' said Harper heading in another direction.

'Not really' said Judy as she screwed her face up and turned her shoulders away from the policemen to indicate that she loathed Louise with every fibre. 'We did not get on very well. She was slap-dash and always late. Not what you expect from Lloyds staff.'

'The gunman picked on you didn't he? He made you go under the desk and bark?' Grace's question hung in the air between the three of them. A poor interrogator might want to step in and ask a more direct question, such as "do you know why he did that?" or "did he do that to humiliate you?" but both police officers knew to hold back and let the witness think, remember and speak.

'Yes, he did pick on me, he called me by my name you know. But it may be because of the badge' she fingered her plastic name badge with a shaking hand as she spoke, 'but I was the only one at the tills, the first one he came to, so that may have been why he picked on me.'

'So you think it was not a premeditated attack on you; just unfortunate' said a smiling Harper. He did not listen to the answer he was already thinking that getting the old lady to bark and hide under the desk was her punishment from a bully showing off.

Grace had already turned away as well as she had been approached by a uniformed policeman. They talked briefly before she turned to Harper.

'Found the bike. No sign of the girl.'

<u>Six</u>

'Where are we going?'

Their car was heading out of Cheltenham towards the motorway at a steady speed. Carl was keeping an eye out for flashing lights but he was confident that things were going to plan currently.

'*We* are going on the motorway as far as the first services. I will leave you there. I will give you some cash for your trouble and I would suggest you find a good hiding spot for it. Then call the police and come back to collect it later. And whilst we talk about calling, can you get your mobile from your handbag and turn it off for me?'

He drove and watched carefully as Louise's Nokia screen lit up then faded away as the power went off. 'Can I have it please? You will get it back eventually.' She handed her phone over and he placed it into the driver's door pocket.

'Would ten grand be OK?' He looked over to her questioningly.

'Pardon' said Louise.

'Would ten grand be OK? If I gave you that would you be able to hide it and wait a while before calling the police. I would just need a bit more time to get up the motorway and, if you had ten grand to stash then would you let me get away?'

'I think I would hand it in as it's the bank's money.'

'I think you'll find it is the customer's money' said Carl lightly. There was a pause as Louise took some courage and added, 'I actually think it's your money now that you have stolen it.'

Carl nodded. 'Fair point, well made. It is my money. If I give some of *my* money to you Louise it would make up for this inconvenience and be a good bonus.' He smiled generously and swept his arm around the car as he said "make up for this inconvenience".

'You used my name. And Judy's and Mr Major's?'

'Well I have been planning this for some time and so I have got to know you all well. I don't like Judy.' Carl wrinkled his nose and shook his head as he said the last line. 'She was a bit of a cow to you.'

'She was fine, just from a different generation.'

'No Louise, she was a bitch and that is why I made her get in her kennel and bark like a bitch. You know she deserved it.'

Louise thought about the presumptuousness of that comment. How the hell does he claim to know how I feel about Judy? But he was right, she did hold a hatred for Judy but had that really led to his shooting at her?

'Did you enjoy the motorcycle ride' he asked. It was strange question and she looked at him in a puzzled way. He looked relaxed. He seat was quite a long way back and he sat askew in the seat so that he was slightly turned towards her. His left hand was on his thigh and the right high on the steering wheel. It was a very open and friendly stance. He had large hands and when he smiled he looked friendly. He was well built she thought and not ugly. She even thought that she may be able to recognise him if she looked at him long enough.

'I can say that it was exciting' she said. He smiled as if he was pleased with the response and looked towards her. Her stance was not open. She had retreated to the far left of the car. Her feet were drawn as far back as the seat squab would allow. Her hands were grasped together on her lap and she was rubbing her thumbs together. Her head was down and she looked at him through the fringe of her hair. She did have great eyes he thought.

'I am sorry to be scaring you. It was unavoidable then, but this may help.' He struggled in his seat and took the gun from under his arm and with a single handed manoeuvre the gun's magazine dropped into his lap. He put the pistol back under his arm and handed Louise the ammunition. It was heavier than she expected.

'Could you put that in your door pocket please?' She was happy to get even that part of the gun out of her hands and return to her submissive position, but the interaction had left her a little more relaxed. He posed a question after a pause, 'do you like working in a bank?'

'It is OK at times. You get some regular customers.'

'Sounds like a laugh a minute.'

'Do you have a job?' Louise offered after a short silence. She suddenly thought that she should pump this guy for lots of information as that would be useful to the police.

'I'm a bank robber.' Louise did not think she would be able to help the police with their enquiries very much with that insight.

'I mean normally; when you're not robbing banks.'

'Louise, I can't tell you much about me at the moment and so I think we had better talk about you.'

'We could sit in silence' she suggested.

'I don't think that's your style' he said with a smile. 'I have been watching you for a while and all the other bank staff. I know you like a chat.' He pulled a disapproving face to admonish her for being a chatterbox. It was like being told off by a kindly geography teacher. She felt herself relax a little more.

Seven

Grace and Harper arrived where the motorbike was leant against the wall and Harper stated the obvious.

'So, up the alley, dumped the bike here and then through the arch onto The Crescent and into a car.' He swivelled on his heel and pointed to the alley and arch in turn picturing the scene in his head. They took some steps into the gloom beneath the arch and looked at the vacant parking space ahead of them. It was like a lost tooth in a grin. Parked cars filled both kerbs and then a gap.

Grace turned and beckoned to a uniformed constable and said 'Can you get knocking on doors please. I want to know who is in and what they saw.'

Grace pulled her radio from her handbag and was told by the control room that the licence plate was registered to a blue Range Rover and that Louise's phone had been switched off when it was in this very locality.

'Can you get the engine or frame number?'

Harper crouched down and then bobbed around as he tried to spot where the plate with the serial number of the bike should be. Where it should have been on the headstock was a bright patch of paintwork with two holes. The plate was gone. Harper bobbed about a little more looking at the engine.

'No VIN plate and the engine number has been scratched over. Hang on though, try this.' Harper was craned over the front wheel and read out a registration number. 'The divvy has left the tax disc on the bike. Of all the stupid things, all that effort to hide the details but he forgot the tax disc.'

'Is it in date? We might as well get him for that as well. Hang on.' Grace listened to control pass back a name and address.

'Carl Richardson and an address in Fairview. Ring any bells?' Harper shook his head and said 'We had best go there before the girl's flat. Won't be five minutes from here.'

They left a constable to contain the site and walked back to Harper's car and Grace rang the station. Standard procedure was to get the press on side and get an appeal for information on the kidnap out as soon as possible. A robber dragging a hostage about was not a thing that went unnoticed. Alternatively, if nobody saw anything then that could indicate that Louise was complicit and was working the inside. She hung up and told Harper that she would need to be at the press conference and ready in two hours.

'What are you going to tell the press?'

'Only that Louise is a hostage, whereabouts unknown, do not approach them if you see them as he is armed and dangerous plus, a general appeal for witnesses for a man hanging around the bank fitting our man's description. And by that time we should have an idea of whether this Carl Richardson is our man.'

They pulled up outside the house of the registered keeper of the motorcycle. It was a small house within a terrace of fifteen. They all faced onto the pavement with their front door being a pace away from the road. They parked right outside and Harper could close his car door and ring the doorbell without moving.

'Do you hope he is in or out?' he said without taking his eyes off the door.

'Well he has a gun and a hostage, so I hope he is out.'

'Interesting. You do think that this is our man

then?'

'You are right Harper.' Grace furrowed her brow as she thought on what Harper had said. 'Female intuition perhaps but yes I think this is our robber's home, and he does seem to be out. I believe that a crime is in progress.'

As Harper stood back, braced himself and lifted his boot he said 'I also believe that a crime is in progress' and aimed a kick at the door. It splinted near the lock and with a shove of the shoulder and further splintering of wood he was able to easily reach the Yale lock and open the door.

They stepped into the room. It was a small house and the internal walls had been removed to make the ground floor open plan. The kitchen was ahead of them, stairs headed up from the far right hand corner and the living space was on their immediate right. The room was spartan but tidy.

'Police' shouted Harper as he went up the stairs two at a time. Clearly the upstairs was as small as the down as he called out 'clear' and then descended.

'First impressions' said Harper.

Grace pursed her lips and started to say what she saw. 'Small television, lots of books.' She walked over to several book cases that filled the right hand wall. She turned her head and looked at the titles. 'The books are important. They are all specifically arranged, but not by title or genre, simply by size, eclectic tastes, novels and literature but a good deal of non fiction. Of the non fiction it seems to be military history and sailing. No chick lit.' She stepped back. Then went further back and then put her hands on her hips. 'This is our man. There is a gap.' She pointed to a two foot space in the top shelf of the bookshelves without turning to look at Harper who had been busy searching the kitchen looking for the waste bin. 'He is single, tidy, fastidious and because he keeps his possessions I would suggest from a lower socioeconomic background. But he has improved himself, probably through education and employment, perhaps in the army, or navy. He is reading widely and is now able to divest himself of his surplus books. He is not hoarding them. He only keeps those he values, the rest I propose he takes to the charity shop. He wouldn't throw a book away. But the gap!' She wagged her finger at the empty bookshelf. 'He has taken the books, a collection, perhaps that usually he keeps there with him. He does not intend to come back. This is our man.'

'I agree' said Harper. Grace turned to look at him for the first time since entering the house and she was smiling, mostly to herself as she had looked at a book shelf and deduced so much, but she was pleased that Harper had agreed with her analysis. She saw that he was holding up in his gloved hand, at eye level, a green paper band with £50 written upon it. It was the wrapper from a brick of bank notes.

'And there are two glasses in the sink, one has lipstick on and I bet the fingerprints of Miss Louise Byrd as well.'

<u>Eight</u>

Louise had decided to keep track of their route as she was certain that the police would want to know it. It had been easy so far as they had headed for the motorway and were headed north. They were not hanging about and had accelerated hard through the slip road bend to merge with and then pass the traffic in the first two lanes of the motorway. Now the speed had ameliorated and they kept station with the other reps' in the fast lane. They were camouflaged and Carl felt only slight unease when a police car flashed by on the opposing carriageway, siren screaming, lights flashing grim faced luminescent clad coppers fixedly staring at the parting of the waves in front of them as they took their power trip. He looked at his watch and then at the clock on the dash. Louise wondered if he had an appointment to keep, perhaps a plane to catch.

'There's a drink in the glove box' offered Carl. Louise did not move other than to turn her head, 'and some Jaffa Cakes.' Still no movement from Louise. 'Can you open them and get one for me?' She opened the glove box and offered the now open box and noted that they felt cold in her hands. Air conditioning in the glove box to keep the Jaffa Cakes cold. Not much worse than melted Jaffas.

'Have one yourself.'

'When are you letting me go?'

'At the next service station, which is not far now. I will leave you with some of the cash. Take your time in hiding it and that will serve us both well. It will give me time to get on and you will be able to come back at a later point and be happy that the cash is safe in the meantime.

Remember that service stations are used to some late night coming-and-goings. Just come back in a few months at a late hour.'

'I did say that I don't want the cash. It's stolen.'

'Well hand it back to the bank or hide it. You did earn it. This,' Carl moved his right hand through an arc above the steering wheel at something that was external to him, 'could not have been a pleasant experience. I don't think the bank will be giving you a reward.' Carl suddenly looked earnest and questioning. 'Do you get a bonus, or overtime for this?'

'I don't think so' replied Louise.

'You should have danger money. A robbery bonus and, I am sorry to say, the police may be questioning you for hours after this. It could be a good earner!'

'You're not suggesting that you are doing me a favour.' Louise kept her voice level but her eyes widened and she took her hands from her lap and opened her palms showing them to the roof of the car. She looked like McEnroe pleading with a line official. Her tone was not completely angry, there was a playful tone, in response to Carl's own.

'No, but every cloud and all that' shrugged Carl 'just saying that' he paused, 'I'm sorry for what I've done to you.' He looked contrite and seemed to be genuine and Louise was puzzled by his show of tender feelings in stark contrast to the brutal machismo shown only a short while before. He looked across the car to her and he saw that she had visibly softened her stance.

'Money is not everything Louise, take that tip from a bank robber. If I did a hundred of these it wouldn't make me a hundred times happier. In fact, it would have the opposite effect. But we can't ignore that we all need money to a larger or smaller degree. Some work hard for it, many inherit it and lots of people are just lucky and I don't mean the lottery, just ideas, right place at the right time, good marriages that kind of thing, but there are lots of people who work hard and gain nothing, many lose it supporting their friends and family and from being in the wrong place at the wrong time. I stole from your bank because I can but I can see that stealing hurts people. Some I think deserve it and others don't. You don't deserve to have a gun shoved in your ribs and being scared by me and all I can do in this short time to justify my wrongdoing is to give you money. That makes me sorry.'

Louise felt that she should say something, and the silence opened up between them, and she jumped into it. 'It's OK.' She smiled weakly and he smiled back mirroring her. 'It stopped today being boring and it's going to be a novel way to clear my student debt.'

'So working in the bank is as dull as I thought, if robbery is needed to break the monotony?'

'Well, Fridays are a problem, usually a bit of a hangover and a struggle to get out of bed are the norm so anything to keep me going on Fridays is good.'

'Well I hope they give you time off to unwind after this' said Carl indicating and moving towards the service slip road.

'I expect life's one big holiday for you though?' wondered Louise aloud.

'Well, staking out and planning take time but I would be lying to suggest that I don't have a heap of down time now. Life will now be a long holiday.' He looked at his watch, then at the clock in the dash and turned into the services and saw two police cars.

<u>Nine</u>

'So where was the glass?' asked Grace. She walked over to the kitchen area and looked in the bowl. The bowl and drainer were empty apart from a neat arrangement of a plate with crumbs, knife with marmalade, a glass, clearly with the remnants of orange juice in, a bowl, traces of milk and cornflakes apparent and finally a single mug.

'Anything else in the bin?'

'Nothing unusual.' He turned the paper band over on the table with the end of a pen. 'Just this. It has a shopping list on the back and looks to have been well scuffed. I would say someone needed to write a list and this paper was at hand.'

'At hand for someone who worked in a bank' added Grace. She thought for a moment and then continued. 'So breakfast for him and a glass of something for her.' Harper held the glass to his nose and looked it over.

'Not juice, can't make out the smell but I would say it was spirits.' The glass was well used and had a crown etched upon it with a half pint plimsoll line. With his free hand Harper opened kitchen cupboards above the sink until he found what he was looking for. He lifted the glass again and held it aloft and in line with the open cupboard.

'It does not match.'

'Come again' said Grace with a smirk.

'The glass with the lipstick, does not match any others.' Grace looked at the small collection of glasses. They were regimented, by size, but in odd numbers as some had clearly fallen during service. He did not have many, just large and small tumblers and glasses with stems. He did have two champagne flutes at the back. All were upside down and spotless. The glass in Harper's hand had clearly been through the washer numerous times and had had a professional life. A pub glass.

'So he has OCD and a stolen glass. We can nail him with that if we can't get armed robbery to stick.' Grace was confused.

Harper tried to clarify 'This', he waved at the glass as he dropped it into a polythene bag, 'does not fit with those' as he nodded to the barrack house of glasses. 'I still think that this will have her prints on, but it does not *belong*. Let's go up stairs.'

'Not when I am on duty Harper' teased Grace looking and then heading for the stairs.

'So you are saying the glass is a plant?'

'It could be ma'am' the formality from Harper made Grace smile, her teasing of the sergeant usually responded in some formality back. She also guessed that he was looking up her skirt as they climbed the stairs and that meant that he was feeling doubly embarrassed.

Harper leaned forward and could see well up his boss's thigh, not as far to have a chance of seeing knickers but a good view and more leg than he normally saw. He straightened his stance as she reached the top of the stairs and his head was level with her arse and he looked for an outline of pants and saw none. He mused that if the stairs were steeper, if he leaned forward more or her skirt was shorter, then maybe, for a split second, he could see more of his boss. She stopped and turned ninety degrees and brought her hand up to her chest and pointed into the room but looked down at Harper's ascent.

'Bedroom' she said raising her eyebrows and

opening her eyes wide with a wicked smile as she stepped over the threshold. Harper stuck his hand in his pocket and rearranged the furniture in his boxers as room was getting tight down stairs.

'Focus man' he mumbled under his breath. 'Yes, the glass and cash wrapper suggest that they are in this together.'

'It is a very clear suggestion, plus she did let him into the rear of the bank' echoed Grace.

'But, the glass does not fit it is not one of his and the wrapper was just on the top of his regular garbage. Very obvious.'

'So you are saying that he covers up some things, such as wearing a mask, but then leaves us obvious pointers?'

'Yes' said Harper cruising his eyes about the bedroom, 'like taking the licence and VIN plate off the bike but leaving the tax disc on. Some concealment, but not enough to stop us getting here.' He turned and looked about the room.

It was not a big room, clearly this floor had a second bedroom and a bathroom taking up space. The bed was large with matching bedside tables. One had a lamp and clock on, the other was bare. The bed was made in a tidy fashion and the whole room was in order. There was a chest of drawers with a television on it and a wardrobe. Pictures of seascapes and landscapes adorned the walls which were painted an off white. You could make the colour difference out as the ceiling was bright white with a glass and steel entwined lampshade. Harper wondered if Louise had spent time on her back in this room looking up at the shade with Carl on top of her and decided that she had not. He went through the chest of drawers first and found some male clothes and in the top drawer some masculine toiletries, if, in his opinion, you can call moisturiser masculine. The wardrobe was similar in that it had some clothes all male but nothing that stood out. The bedside table had a drawer with lots of odds and ends plus, massage oil but no condoms.

'What do you see Harper?'

'I don't think she has been here or certainly does not stay here. Nothing feminine at all. He has packed to leave and left the clothes he rarely wears and has left warm clothes. He isn't going skiing either' stated Harper after a look under the bed and seeing a snow board and a bundle of ski gear. 'And he hopes to score as he has taken his jonnies.'

He walked to the far side of the bed 'and why make the bed but leave the washing up, unless the bed would show a single man slept here, yep. I would stake my pension that she has never been here.' And with that Harper opened the other bedside table and found a pair of girls panties, tampons, makeup, plenty of general girly bric-a-brac and there staring back at him was a Lloyds bank identity card with a picture of Louise Byrd on.

Ten

Carl visibly tensed as he saw the police cars. One was a Volvo estate, twin crewed and full to the gunnels with the usual motorway cop paraphernalia. The sides were emblazoned with chequerboard fluorescence depicting the game of chess, chase and chance the police play so well. The other car was a top end BMW, darkest blue and without obvious police markings other than a cornucopia of aerials, two rear view mirrors and extra lights that were flashing in a dizzying pattern The pattern initially seemed random, but with some hypnotic staring it fell into a circular pattern, drawing you into a whirlpool, at the centre of which, was a rolling LED display of 'Caution POLICE.' The two cars were some distance away, well within the car park and facing in opposite directions Volvo towards the entrance and the BMW facing away. They were drawn closely together so that the drivers could converse through their lowered windows.

Carl surveyed his mirrors, a family in a Focus behind him and then a rep mobile barrelling up the slip after that. He decelerated more to allow the family to catch up glanced a look at Louise. 'Don't make a move. I will be letting you go and driving away shortly.'

'OK' replied Louise, who had been contemplating drumming on the windows and waving, but why chance that if Carl was going to let her go anyway? She looked at the gap where the door lock should have been. "Sit tight" she thought but she looked towards the police. The drivers were talking together but the passenger of the marked car was looking at the traffic. She wondered if they were looking for them.

Carl swung off into the car park at the first

chance he got. The chances that the police would be looking for them were remote, unless they had a witness of the bike-to-car switch. If that had happened then the police would not be looking for *this* car. He looked for an urgent move from either car and saw none. He headed towards the back of the parking area where the caravans, lorries and dog walkers frequented. He turned in between two artics and stopped, switching off the engine.

'We have a problem' he said solemnly. 'I did not expect the police to actually be here.' He turned in his seat by bending his knee and pushing back against his own door. He raised his hands in an act of submission and took on a pleading look. 'If I let you go here, would you promise not to talk to the police for at least fifteen minutes so that I have a head start?'

Before Louise had a chance to reply Carl had a change of heart. 'I don't think that would be long enough though' he said to himself letting his hands fall onto his lap.

'I could wait longer?' offered Louise in a quiet voice and she could see Carl thinking.

'I was hoping that you would spend some time hiding cash, then get someone to call the police, wait for them to arrive, then they would ask some questions and be after me in about thirty minutes. You wouldn't be able to hang around here having coffee and a danish waiting thirty minutes. And that BMW looks like a swift pursuit car.' Carl was looking down toward his hands, but then raised his eyes and took on a serious air. 'OK. A favour to ask, I could get the gun out and start making threats but, I would rather just make a request. I was going to leave you here but I can take you a little further with me and let you out' he paused making a calculation, 'I'm heading into Wales and can let you out en route, miles from any coppers, so' he rushed on 'sorry to do this, to ask this, but are you OK to come on further with me?'

Louise's mouth fell slightly open. A flash of being asked out for the first time and thinking of her surprise of being thought of as attractive went through her mind. It was Hobson's choice. To say "no" to an armed robber and piss him off, or say "yes" and get taken on to god knows where. She was not feeling threatened at present. He seemed to have changed into someone who was almost submissive and meek.

'OK' she said, and then in response to his gentle smile, 'but not much further.'

'OK' said Carl. I will let you out in an hour or so and with that he turned himself around facing forward again and started to pull things from the car's cubby holes and his own pockets. 'This is where I try to lay a false trail.'

Louise watched as he pulled out a mobile and initially she thought he would make a call but he put it within a plastic bag and then got out of the car. Once outside Carl also fished Louise's phone from his pocket and placed it into the bag. He walked leisurely to the front of the car and surveyed the lorries, both cabs looked empty and Carl checked the decals upon the doors. One was a national carrier with only a serial number and phone number which was an 0800 number but the other was much more to his liking. The name inferred an owner driver outfit with a Glasgow address. Parked in the northbound services and looking laden, he could assume the rig was on the way home. Carl zip locked his plastic bag and through the plastic pressed the on buttons on both phones and the bag lit up in an eerie blue and green glow as the two phones tried to outshine the other. Now all he needed was somewhere to conceal it. He walked back towards the car and Louise and then ducked beneath the trailer and pushed the packet through one of the many diamond shaped holes in the trailer chassis. He kept bent double and swung back to the car door, opened it and in a fluid movement, put the car in gear, started the engine, let out the clutch, pulled off and let the momentum swing the door closed. They accelerated away from their phones as they tried to find their local base station and get a connection. He watched the two police cars reduce in size in his rear view mirror. He was surprised to see two, normally there was only one stationed there.

Eleven

Grace and Harper were in the park getting ice cream. Cheltenham is a town of parks, there is always one nearby and an ice cream, on a park bench, on a spring day was idyllic and something that Harper loved. Harper, in times of trouble would recite "Making mistakes makes you wise and hard work makes you clever". He had made a mistake in his early days in CID when he suggested to his then boss to adjourn to the pub for a beer and to think over the case. He knew he had made a mistake through the look in his superior's face. Colour rushed into it, his whole body swelled, his mouth dropped open with incredulity. Harper remembered thinking over what he had said as he could see he was at the wrong end of a flame thrower "Go to the pub and have a chat shall we" roared his boss "we have a body on the ground and you suggest we get on the piss. I think you have been watching too much of the Sweeny and not watching the way this country is going son…etc". Harper could not remember the details from then on but he was sure that national service and lack of moral fibre was mentioned. And so the lesson was learnt and now as the bosses pass through his care and the time comes to reflect on the evidence, propose theories and to generally get out to the car and office he suggests an ice cream. He did try suggesting coffee for a while but another boss complained about the "cappuccino culture, don't they have mugs of tea in Cheltenham" and so innocuous ice cream it was. He did feel that a beverage or in the case of ice cream, confectionary was required in these meetings to inject some informality and to allow the boundaries of rank to be highlighted.

'I'll get these ma'am.'

'No, they will be on me.' They were stood shoulder to shoulder peering down through the clear sliding lid of the ice cream freezer.

'But if I get them I can stick them on my expenses and you can sign them off ma'am.'

'Well I think it is my turn as you got them last time and you never put them on your expenses.'

'Well if you're sure, I will have' and sliding the glazed door open Harper announced 'Choc Chip, I will make a call and see you outside?'

They reconvened outside, both of them with phones to ears. Harper was sat at a small metal table, on an uncomfortable folding chair, with the elbow of the hand holding the phone pressed onto his notebook so that he could write in it with his free hand. Grace had her head canted heavily to one side to press phone to ear and have her hands free to carry a small tray with her breakfast of ice cream and coffee.

Grace sat. They both clicked off their phones and started on the ice creams and after a pause to savour the flavour and for Grace to put on sunglasses and tip her head up to the sun they started.

'So where are we' opened Grace?

'Firstly, ma'am, I am coming round to the inside job.'

'Hmm', was Grace's reply, partly as the ice cream and sun was lovely and partly as she knew Harper actually wanted to continue.

'Her possessions are at his house and he seems to either have luck, or a talent for this. The bank has had a tally and he has got close to £100k. They say they were stocking up for bank holiday and were holding more cash than normal. I did check and the Byrd girl would have known that would happen. And we can not escape the fact that she did let him in.'

'But at gunpoint.'

'Well, yes but I think that is also important ma'am as I have had a quick ring to Oscar to see if he could suggest any potential armed robbers that I hadn't thought of and he came up with a blank.'

'So if the two oracles of the constabulary, with your encyclopaedic minds of all the wrong uns in Gloucestershire can't put anyone in the frame you then think it must be an inside job?'

'Well yes ma'am. Between Oscar and me I think we have met or nicked all the known armed robbers who live here. So if he's an outsider then he knows the roads well. If he's an outsider then he was lucky with the bank and the haul. And if he's an outsider then he was lucky that she was late and let him in.'

'But she had a gun to her head Harper. You would have let him in if he had a gun to your head. Is she involved or just in the wrong place at the wrong time? We need to get a link between the two of them.'

'A better link than her knickers at his house? I would say they seemed well linked already.'

'But that seems a little odd though Harps, would you go out with a girl and leave your boxers at her place?' Grace looked over her tub of ice cream at her sergeant and waited for an answer.

'Don't wear boxers ma'am, more of a Y front man; for the support.'

'Too much detail and I don't care about the

content of the pants, just, as a girl, I am not sure I would leave my pants at a fella's house. Clothes yes, but not just my pants.'

'Maybe they were a trophy then' suggested Harper.

Grace let her plastic spoon fall towards the table as she looked to the sky and rolled her eyes, 'what a lovely thought, racks of knickers to remember his lady friends by, no I just think it was odd.'

'But is it that odd to have a spare? I know that my wife, has on occasion, carried spares?' Harper was visibly blushing at discussing the goings on in his wife's briefs, or not so brief, pants.

Grace decided to ride his embarrassment 'Well you are right, periods can be anything but regular and deposited semen has a nasty habit of giving in to gravity at inopportune moments. And the joy of a penis, you men don't get our troubles with leaks after a cough, sneeze or of wetting yourself laughing. So there is a lot going on inside this girl's knickers that may necessitate carrying a spare. I think you best ask her colleagues and her parents about that.' Grace bit down on her ice cream spoon to try to smother a giggle as Harper chased a choc chip in his tub and frowned.

'Well it will hang together as an inside job due to the hard evidence. You and Oscar may be the oracle but you're not infallible or omnipotent. Things clearly point to them being in each other's company and at present we have no idea where the hell they are. I have put the press conference on hold. We will look stupid saying she was kidnapped and a hostage if she is actually the mastermind of the thing.

<u>Twelve</u>

'I will let you out soon', restated Carl as he concentrated on navigating a roundabout. Louise was familiar with this area and was interested in his heading, but he surprised her (and she expected, the police), by heading back the way he came. After a short, fast, southward journey they swung off onto the M50 and headed for Wales. The M50 is a glorified dual carriageway running flat and straight past market towns across the floodplains of the Avon and Severn. The ridgeback of the Malvern Hills erupted from the green pastures on their right and rose in growing peaks like steps to heaven itself. This outlier shows only as a precursor of the black mountains of Wales beyond and the steady even escarpment of the Cotswolds before, as if the flat lands between the two had decided to liven things up with an exhibition in what hills should look like.

Carl looked at his watch, the clock in the car and all the mirrors and went for a sweet from the door pocket. He offered one to Louise, who accepted.

'What I can do is, once the motorway ends, we will get onto a back road and what I plan to do is stop and eat and I can then drive on alone. I expect that you will have a bit of a walk to raise the alarm and I am sorry about that, but I still need some time to get away.' He looked over to Louise and seemed to be looking for some validation on what he said.

'That's OK', she replied. 'You keep looking at your watch' she added, but only after a pause. Carl instinctively looked again at it.

'Yes' was absently said 'I have an appointment' he said with a smile. 'Some things just won't wait. I can't tell you more as it is part of the getaway.'

'Sorry, I shouldn't have asked.'

'That's fine.' There was an awkward silence and then Carl looked over to Louise.

'So, tell me about you. I wish I could tell you more about me' he said with a shrug of resignation, 'but given the hostage situation I had better not.'

'Surely you can tell me something?'

After a lengthy silence Carl started. 'Well, I was in the forces for a good few years and then left with a knee injury. Parachute jump. Well the jump was fine it was more the landing. Civilian life was dull in comparison to the travel and camaraderie. Normal jobs had no purpose or reason.' He looked over towards Lou again with sadness in his eyes. 'But it was the mates that I missed. You spend years living with, working with and being with', as he said "being with" his hand left the steering wheel and he placed his first finger and thumb together and moved them forcibly back at the steering wheel as if he was reaching out through the windscreen, perhaps beckoning to something that he wanted to return to him. He had a grimace on his face. 'So many good mates in a cocoon of olive green that you just disconnect with reality.' With that he slid his hands around the steering wheel as if he was checking that it was really there. 'And when you are out, I saw that civilian life had nothing to offer me. I saw that I couldn't work nine to five. I didn't want a dead end job, I wanted to live life, as I have seen the alternative. Up close.' He looked across to emphasise the next statement. 'Close friends have died. Bang. Gone. Nothing left. And so I knew I wanted to enjoy the world and the time that I have left. And so, I am sorry to say, I robbed your bank so that I can have the cash. I don't need to work now. I have sold everything that I had, car, house, possessions and with this' he gestured behind him and she knew he meant the holdall behind them 'then I will have enough to live a good life travelling.' He smiled a contented smile towards her.

'That sounds like a lonely existence' Lou quietly said.

'Well, as I planned this and weighed that up, that was the downside of being on the run. But I don't have a great deal of faith in the police solving crimes and so I expect they will eventually give up looking and then I will be able to settle down someplace warm.'

'You won't miss England?' said Louise raising a hand towards the windows to show Carl the kaleidoscope of Herefordshire landscapes.

'Yes, I might, but I suspect that I will be able to get back into the UK in the future. Have you travelled much Louise?'

'The States, Greece and France all on holidays with the folks or friends, oh and Italy skiing.'

'How good is your French?' asked Carl with some interest.

'O level, grade A and I got by during my French exchanges, why do you ask?' Carl started and then stopped himself. Lou guessed that he may have been about to give something away. A hide out in a chateau perhaps. She risked a question. 'How is your French?'

'Not bad.' He seemed to think for while then continued as if he had decided to relent to an inner voice. 'I had a girlfriend who I met whilst I was serving in France. It was a wanky; sorry rubbish,' (Lou thought it odd that he apologised for saying "wanky" but was happy to point guns at people) 'attachment with NATO and so I spent six months in Paris.'

'Paris in Love' playfully added Louise opening her eyes wide in Carl's direction. She was enjoying listening to him open up a little and she wanted to pursue this line of enquiry.

'Well, yes it was. Paris was much better than the job and without so many of the Company around me, I then wanted company. Cheryl provided that and showed me the sights and taught me the language.'

'How did you meet?' Lou had swivelled around a little more and was looking closely at Carl to see how he would react to the personal questioning.

'She was attached to the staff at the embassy and we met through work and...' his voice drifted off a little and his head fell to the left as he looked into his memories 'she was lovely. But, she became a bit possessive and the wheel fell off.'

'What do you mean by that?'

'Well' started Carl, looking a bit sheepish, 'I did not cover myself in glory in the way it ended. As I say, she was possessive and I wanted a night out with some of the lads from the embassy. We seldom went out and it was not like we were on the pull or anything but she was paranoid and wanted me in by twelve and said I should not go clubbing. She was half right as it was 11:45 when I called a cab from this club. I dialled the number for the taxi firm the embassy always used and when they answered I said "Hi can I have a taxi" and they said "Carl"? Now we could ring this firm and talk English but I was surprised that they recognised my voice. I was a bit taken aback and carried on and said again "Can I have a taxi?" They then said "Are you in a club" and I began to think that this was a little odd that the taxi firm knew who I was and where I was, but to put a top on it they launched into French and called me a bastard and other things I could not make out and then they threw the phone down. As I looked at the phone in some wonderment it dawned on me that I have misdialled and had rung Cheryl instead of the taxi firm.'

Louise spat out a laugh, 'oops.'

'Yes, she was not pleased and the boys thought it was hilarious.'

'You didn't tell them as well?' Louise continued to laugh.

'Well it was a drunken mistake. I did leave and go to face the music and was at her place for twelve. I found all my stuff in a pile outside her flat. So that was that. I made an orderly retreat to the barracks and never saw her again.'

'Oh no, never saw her again, that is terrible!' smirked Louise.

'But it was such a relief' Carl stole a look across to Louise and grinned at her laughing at his misfortune 'you must've had boyfriends that you were relieved to end it with, and getting slung out for an honest mistake was a good way to escape. As I picked up my gear from her garden I literally heaved a sigh of relief as I went on my way. And a few weeks later I was back in England.'

'That is a terrible way to end a relationship' giggled Louise.

'*She* ended it by slinging me out; in a foreign country too!' pleaded Carl with a broad smile on his face. 'Anyhow, time for lunch I think.'

He started to decelerate and shook his head slowly 'and I had a long walk home too.'

<u>Thirteen</u>

The ice cream was finished with judicious scraping of the tub by Harper who then neatly arranged the spoon and lid back onto the carton. Grace left the dregs and tossed the detritus into the bin and fished out a Wet Wipe to clean up with. In these moments of husbandry she decided the plan of action.

'We need to identify where they are heading. If she is going forcibly or voluntarily we still need to know where. He is the key and so we need to know what his plan is.'

'Why is he the key?'

'His age, or more precisely, her age. I just think that even if it is her plan he will be leading the getaway. He has ridden the bike and I suspect is driving the car. Let's focus on that then; Harps call the DVLA and check if he has a car registered to him, or her for that matter. If so then get the details out.'

'Won't the car be stolen?'

'I don't think that you and the oracle are omnipotent, but I do think you know your local crims. He did not steal the motorbike and you don't think he is a regular customer of ours and so if he needs a car for this, I don't think he would have stolen one.'

The mobile rang and Harper had a look at the number before answering.

'Interesting, where? In which direction? Is anyone on that? OK, just hold.' Harper put the phone on the table and made no attempt to put the call on hold or mute the receiver. 'We seem to have a break ma'am, their mobiles, both of them have been switched on and are heading northbound on the M5, they are close to the M6.

West Midlands are offering assistance so what do you want to do?'

'Both phones, that is convenient?' Grace seemed to think then picked up her own phone whilst leafing through her Moleskin then dialled.

'Best to ring the kidnapee and offer assistance.'

Harper picked up his phone and asked the caller to continue to hold and Grace and he locked eyes in a mirror like pose, both intent on the other but also concentrating on the phone.

'Ansa phone' said Grace hanging up and dialling again. After a wait she added 'and on his. I don't think that they are with the phones, this is just too convenient, but get West Mids onto this and see if they can retrieve the phones. Let them know that I had no answer and they can ring themselves."

Harper relayed the information as they walked back to the car and Grace said, more to herself than to Harper, 'back to the station and let's get the team mobilised and then to her place. I feel a bit of leg work coming on. Nice ice cream.'

Fourteen

Carl pulled across the westbound carriageway and into a small car park next to a public toilet. No other cars were there and when their engine was off the noises of rural Monmouthshire became audible. The wind in the oaks of the valley behind them, the twittering of numerous birds and the pastoral bleat of a lamb. It would have been idyllic without the occasional tyre roar and the kidnaper with a gun. Carl came around to open Lou's door, which she may have found to have been gentlemanly, if he hadn't removed the lock to prevent her escape. Once out to the car things became less adversarial and he had left the gun either in the car or hidden on his person. She stretched and headed towards the ladies.

'Louise, I just wanted to say that I can leave you close to here. If you are happy to eat then, we can sort the cash out and I will be off. If that is OK with you?'

The "if that is OK with you" was a bit of a shock and took her off guard.

'Yeah, food would be good; that would be great.'

They stood nodding at one another and Carl backed off to the gents 'OK, see you shortly' and they went their separate ways and were alone.

Louise thought that this maybe a time to run for it, but she did need the loo and if he was going to leave her here anyway, then she might as well get fed and have some cash. As she used the toilet she thought of the practicalities of money laundering large sums through an account and decided that it would not be an issue as she only had to identify a dormant account and make use of that. She finished up with a good wash and looked in the metal mirror. Public toilets. He had just asked her permission, asked her if it was OK to eat here and to sort the cash out. A stark contrast to the gun toting demands of a few hours ago. She began to think that she was with a bipolar madman and that she should make a run for it. But then thought she may have missed her chance. She headed outside tentatively. Carl had moved the car so that the passenger door waited just a few steps from the exit.

'There is a lay-by just up that road, so that we get away from the main road. Away from the noise,' Carl added the last bit for clarification. He was bending his head down towards the gear stick so that he could see Lou. She smiled at him and felt little threat from him now and she was hungry. She got in.

The lay-by was just up the road. It was on a minor road leading up behind the toilets, up a side valley. You could guess that it led to a farm, populated by rotund welsh farmers, hale and hearty, ruddy faced and full of lamb and cheese. The road headed uphill and bent with the contours and the main road was soon lost to their hearing. The two of them sat on the boot sill, between them was a well packed cool box. The top layer held drinks, sandwiches and fruit. Below that Lou could see more practical things, milk, butter, bread, eggs. Also in the boot were boxes and bags, it looked like Carl was moving house.

Carl offered Lou the choice of sandwiches; two packets, shop bought, one of which was her sandwich of daily choice and coffee from a thermos was produced as she tucked in. She looked over the fecund countryside, oaks of startling size dressing the valley sides and lush grass dotted with sheep and crossed with grey dry stone walls crossing the valley floor. She expected a stream to be nearby that had tirelessly worked its way through the landscape to design and draw the scene before her. It would have been perfect apart from the grey sky and growing wind that brought a chill that stroked the uppermost branches.

'Looks like rain' said Carl as he put the lid on the cool box after extracting a pair of cereal bars and handing one to Lou and replenishing her coffee, 'best to finish off the thermos.' He stood with his head erect and looked to be studying the sky with an astute eye. Lou wondered what he was looking for within the clouds.

A cold breeze flowed down the valley and caused Lou to move into the shelter of the hatchback boot lid and she saw the rain advance down the valley. They sipped the last of the coffee and she pulled her cardy closer around herself and let out a shudder.

'OK' said Carl with some finality and raising a hand to point higher up the valley. 'There is a farm up there in about a mile and you are half that distance to the main road, your choice where to go.' He delved deep into the recesses of the boot and scooped out two bundles of cash. Bound, wrapped and sealed. *Normal* people would have had bulging eyes and mouth open at this point but the familiarity of large amounts of paper cash to Lou robbed her of the drama as Carl handed ten thousand pounds to her. She held it in front of her in both her hands. The rain intensified from a gentle drum on the roof to a more chaotic rumble. The contract had seemed to have been made between them. 'I would hide that somewhere and come back for it when;' Carl paused and made a vague gesture with his head and subtly moved to stand directly in front of her, 'when it is all over. Anyway, I had better get on my way.' He reached up towards the hatchback that was providing some semblance of shelter but reached out a hand to Lou's shoulder to keep her under the shelter of the car and to keep her in his own shelter as Carl said with real sincerity 'I am sorry for scaring you, dragging you here. It must have been scary.' Lou let out an involuntary exhalation of mirth at that understatement.

'It was a bit of a shock' she said with her own understatement and then carried on without thinking to add 'but it has been OK.'

He rubbed her shoulder and smiled down at her in a real reflection of a father at a proud daughter. She had no choice but to smile as she gazed up at him. A gust of wind brought a smattering of rain into their little sphere of shelter and Carl's guiding hand moved Lou and he moved himself more to windward to shelter her and then he took his hand away as he reacted to the fact that he was touching her. He had spent some of that day holding her, lifting her, pushing and pulling her, but the gently guiding hand was the touch that he quickly retreated from.

'Well, I just wanted to say sorry' and then he took his gaze from her and looked over his shoulder into the heart of the valley and the rain. 'I would give you a lift, but I need a good head start to get on my way.' His hand remained on the boot lid and as he moved away and pulled it down Lou moved from the shelter and felt the cold of the wind and rain. They both looked at the prospect. 'I don't have a coat that I can lend to you; sorry.' Carl looked away from her and down at the ground, wrinkles appeared on his forehead as he tussled with a thought. He had a brief struggle with his conscience and made a decision. He decided to carry on and settled on the course to take. He knew what he wanted to do.

'Alternatively, you can stick with me for a bit

longer. I need to move on now but I can look out for somewhere to leave you when the rain passes?'

The now bedraggled, sodden sheep continued to ruminate over clover as water dripped through their fleeces. Lou simply thought, *I'm going to get soaked.* She thought of the heat and shelter of the car. She looked at Carl and weighed up freedom from a potential nutter or getting soaked and frozen in the middle of nowhere.

She looked down at the cash cupped in her hands and she thought about the option to stay or go. The fear of uncertainty should have remained with her but it had subsided as they took on the more mundane tasks of travel, eating and chatting. She no longer feared for her life, if she ever really had. The demented thug who robbed banks had been true to his word to her. He had not harmed her since they had got away from Cheltenham, he seemed remorseful for the bruises and shock that he had caused and she stood with the cash in her hands. The cash he had said he would hand onto her. At this point, as she began to feel the rain wetting her hair and the cold pervade her cardigan she also made a decision. She decided between the exposure to the raw elements or the warmth of a car. These thoughts raced imperceptibly through her mind as she simply replied 'OK.' She hated the cold.

Fifteen

Armed robbery will garner a large police response. Kidnapping would also produce a good response. Add the two, plus the media interest and the resources of the Gloucestershire Constabulary were at the complete disposal of DI Grace Taylor. In the first few hours of closely chasing their quarry Taylor had not been able to corral these resources but at this juncture she had stepped back and delegated orders like a tree would shed leaves in winter. She believed the mantra of her father that capturing information could lead to the capture of the criminal and as the physical trail cooled the intelligence led investigation was brought to the boil. As the day progressed she and Harper convened informally with a coffee. There would soon be a much more formal meeting with the Chief Constable and the massed ranks of the media to face.

'Her house still quiet?'

'Yes ma'am we have a body on watch and all is quiet there.'

'Latest on the phones?'

'Still mobile on the M6, continuing North. Still being shadowed but until they stop we can't pinpoint them. They will have to stop for a piss at some point soon ma'am.'

'And still no other phones traced for them.' Harper replied with a firm shake of the head.

'I will see Carl's work colleague,' she turned a leaf in her Moleskin and read 'James Munro, in an hour and see if that leads to where he would be heading. See if we can get any more about him.'

'I did get their bank account information looked

at by PC Harrison and I would not say that either of them were skint. He had a forces pension and savings but no mortgage. The most interesting things are in the last six months where he has debited most of his savings. £30K six months ago and the rest as smaller amounts. Her balance is much more modest but she had savings and income exceeded expenditure nicely.'

'What was her overall balance?' Harper pushed the print outs about on the desk and flatly stated £8,300 at the end of last month.'

'And was she withdrawing cash like he was?'

'No ma'am, all looks consistent from one month to the next.'

'OK so he may have been getting his money out before this disappearing act, he was planning ahead, but she wasn't?' She had not meant it to be a question but it did come out that way. They still need to decide if this was a job with inside assistance.

'But her account is in her own bank ma'am, I wonder if the bosses would notice her removing all her funds, so she kept them where they were.'

'Hmm' was Grace's response to that. 'Still inconclusive. What was the story with the military record?' She had left Harper to sort that out as the plethora of acronyms would only have annoyed her.

'Well, ma'am' started Harper pulling back his lips and straightening himself up in preparation for telling the tale. He started to break into a slight smile as he shuffled his files. 'He was a good soldier. Joined at seventeen, it seems he started his A' levels but joined the Marines before they were completed. Passed out well in his cohort and served with some distinction in his eighteen years service. Medals awarded for daring doos in Ireland.

Medical discharge, with a knee injury, at the rank of sergeant. The military are aware that he then worked as a contractor with other ex-marines in the Middle East and that ties in with the bank records that we have. Well paid work. His employers were not very forthcoming on what he was up to, but that can be expected. Nothing of note or too extraordinary though. The guy you are going to see later James Munro served with him as a Marine, is now a club bouncer and his service record was very ordinary, nothing sinister.'

'And talking of records nothing on our records on any of these names, including Louise?'

'That is right ma'am, we have had time to check everyone and they are conspicuously clean. Apart from the one who is the bank robber and potential kidnapper.'

'And I have seen the report on the prints on that glass from his house, they are confirmed as her prints. So she knew Carl and had been at his house.' Grace waved a sheet of A4 as she said that and then laid it on the table and pushed her hands into her hair and also put her elbows on the table holding her head as if to keep in the colliding and circulating thoughts.

'Yes she did know him well enough to have her pants at his house' conceded Harper.

'Well you can check your suspicious trail of the pants with your wife and see if she can shed light on that mystery later. So she *is* a suspect *and* the victim currently.' As they were in her office and no one else was around Grace allowed her head to fall onto the desk and Harper looked at the ball of blond hair and heard it say in exasperation 'What shall I tell the media, and the Chief?'

'I think that all you can do is treat her as a victim of kidnapping at present and get the media to spread her photo and the story as widely as possible.'

'But Harps', she lifted her head and pushed her hair back from her face, a movement that he knew she would have made all of her life, 'that means I am going to have to sit next to the blubbing parents on the ten o'clock news as they appeal for their little angel to be set free just when we might have to slap the cuffs on her for armed robbery.'

'I don't think it will make the ten o'clock news ma'am' said Harper in a misplaced but serious way. 'I can't see that you can go on TV and say that she is a suspect just cos we found her pants at his house. If they are her pants, we didn't them checked for DNA. Do you think we should have?'

'God no Harper. Leave the girl's pants alone. If they are not hers then we know the ID badge is. You're fixated with pants. We need to nail down their relationship though.'

'So we need to find out if he was in her pants?' Before Grace had a chance to find a witty, or shitty response to that, the door was knocked and both officers turned to look at the policewoman whose head had appeared at the jamb.

'Sorry to disturb sarge but you said to let you know when the neighbour called, he has just got in and will be waiting for you to visit.'

As one they rose and began to gather belongings.

Sixteen

They drove in silence for a while. Louise had expected, for some reason, that they would return to the main roads but the roads became smaller and narrower. Their average speed dropped and Carl referred to his watch regularly. The rain persisted and intensified, drumming a tattoo into the roof and windows. The wipers pushed and splashed the water from their view. At some points the biggest trees reached out from both shoulders of the road so that their boughs arched like outstretched arms across the camber of the road and entwined above their heads. The tree tunnel provided a shield from the rains and as they swished under their canopy the pummelling of the rain lifted and fell in a wave of noise to match the waves of water. Louise was, due to the soporific nature of the post lunch warmth of the car, feeling more relaxed than she should. She was still a hostage, being kidnapped and taken towards a fate that was unknown to her. She really should not be dozing off. Carl was unaware that she was dropping off. Had he noticed he would have let her sleep, but his concentration was elsewhere.

'I am glad that I didn't leave you out in this.' He looked over towards her gestured out towards the grey weather. He bent towards the wheel and strained to look up between the trees and seek out a break in the cloud and found none. 'It was forecast, I should have foreseen…' he trailed off and looked at his watch and continued after a pause 'but I planned to leave you there' another waved gesture, this time over his shoulder. He turned to snatch a look at her and caught her eye and held it for a second. That fleeting look provided some emphasis to his next statement. 'I can't leave you on this road Louise. This road leads to where I am going.' His oversimplification seemed to frustrate him and he sought a better vocabulary. 'I mean, back there' he pointed behind himself with his thumb, as if he were doing the Lambeth walk, 'there the police would have lots of options on where I could be heading. I would expect them to follow the main road, to think of the ferry ports perhaps, lots of small roads and properties. But on this road' he held the steering wheel gently in the crook of his thumb and first finger and pointed with all his fingers, 'this road really only goes to one place; one thing and so if I leave you here, then they will find me really easily.' Louise began to wonder where this conversation was leading and with that realisation she began to tense herself. The subconscious flinch was received and understood by Carl, 'but don't worry, I don't plan to leave you in a ditch, I just mean that I will need to keep you' he struggled to say the word and seemed to flinch himself '*prisoner* a little longer.'

'How much longer?'

'Well, you will see in a while, but I promise that I will keep you safe and let you go when I know that you are OK and in a place that won't give me away.' Louise noticed that he had not looked towards her as that promise was made but she gave some consideration to the fact that the small roads they had been travelling seemed voluminous to the road on which they now travelled. It had that great and distinguishing feature of the unclassified road; grass was growing through the asphalt in the middle of the road. Perhaps roads were like venerable professor types with eccentricities that extended to plumes of ear, nasal and eyebrow hair appearing where little or no hair should be. The grass brushed the sump as they crawled down the track and this new navigation was taking Carl's attention. They pulled to a stop as the last of the rain fell through the leaves of the trees crowding the road and the afternoon sun made an appearance. They had arrived.

Seventeen

The police work on surprise. It's a perk of the job sometimes. That look of astonishment as a criminal, when caught red handed, looks over their own shoulder to see who had just dropped a hand onto it. Thrusting a warrant card into a face of an obnoxious felon who then struggles to focus on the fact that they have been caught in the act. Those were the best; shocking the criminals who thought they were invincible, above the law, beating the system and seeing them realise that their Achilles heel had been found, it had brought them down and they had been beaten by the system. It's not always a perk of the job. Sometimes they had brought surprise to a home, not by kicking in the door, but by ringing the bell. And waiting patiently for an answer and hoping that a child did not provide that answer. As when that happened they would have to ask "hello is daddy in?" They would ask for daddy as they knew that mummy was never going to answer any door again and they were there to let daddy know that. And then they would walk away onto the next job, leaving a family who may never move on.

But this look of surprise was not on that league but Mr Parkinson, the neighbour of an armed robber, was looking shocked and repeated his question.

'You don't want to come in?'

'No Mr Parkinson, we want you to come next door into Mr Richardson's house.' They stood back and moved down the terrace followed by a flustered Mr Parkinson who was unexpectedly now looking for his keys and shoes. He gave up on the latter when realising that he was holding up the forces of law and order and made the journey to his neighbour's house in three tippy-toe movements of his slippers.

The terrace wasn't long, five houses facing directly onto the pavement. And the back of a primary school facing back across the narrow street. Carl Richardson, AKA the bank robber had the end terrace and no-one seemed to know him apart from his next door neighbour. Who now came through the door into his neighbour's house.

'We wanted you to come in and look around with us Mr Parkinson as we have some things that we need help with.' Grace counted them off on her fingers. 'We need some background on Mr Richardson, who his friends were, what he did, as much as you can tell us, everything you can tell us. Most importantly is where he went, we need to know where he might be. Being here may jog your memory and provide some inspiration. We are told that you knew him well?'

'Not really well, no. I didn't know he was a criminal' that final word was spat out with some distaste. Mr Parkinson did not look like an accomplice to an armed robber. Perhaps he could be robin to a batman though. They ushered him to sit down.

'But you did know him?' prompted Harper.

'Yes, when I moved here he knocked my door and introduced himself. We had a few beers and got on well enough to have a few nights out in the local. We both work away a bit, he was in the forces you know?' The officers nodded back at that dumb question. 'And I am in computer sales which takes me away. He was a nice guy, despite being a mercenary. We never talked about his business, I suppose you call it that. I would sometimes ask where he was going, or had been; out of politeness…like he would be asking me what I had been doing, but he would just tell me straight that he would rather not discuss that. But it was not in a sad way, I didn't get the feeling he was doing anything traumatic or had shell shock, or that post drama thing, he just kept that business to himself. I don't know if you know about GCHQ here in Cheltenham?' The officers didn't even bother to nod back at that dumber question, 'but people there can't talk about what they do even if it's dull computer stuff, so him not being able to talk about it did not seem too unusual. But then he stopped doing it and was here a lot more, he said he was loaded and didn't want to keep doing that and was looking for more settled work. I thought he could work at my place as he came across as a bright bloke and he had a real can-do attitude.' He became animated as he said "can-do attitude" and leaned more forward in the armchair and made speech marks in the air as he said it. 'You got the impression that he would be able to get anything to happen,' his eyes opened wide 'through force of personality or something, but when I talked of working in software, in an office, learning about computers, he just laughed. He could not settle on what he wanted to do. He said he would work for himself and whenever I asked what that was going to be he would say that he was,' (more speech marks in the air were made) 'waiting for an idea. He worked at a club as a bouncer from time to time but he said that was a favour for a mate and loathed the drunkenness of it. He did not moan about much, but he was a machine with fitness and tidiness, order, discipline and stuff, so seeing pissed up students trying to pick fights annoyed…no that's not the word…it *depressed* him.' Parkinson's eyes flashed between them and he spread a hand out to each of them, with his hand up like a stop sign 'don't get the wrong idea of him when I said annoyed as he was a big tough guy, but I never saw him angry or thought for a second that he would do anything like this. He had self control. Not a bad bone in his body.' With that assurance he sat back in the armchair.

'Did you know he had a gun Mr Parkinson?' Grace asked.

'God no!' He was back on the edge of his seat his voice raising as he raised himself 'I would have rung you, no no, he was a straightforward guy.'

Harper took his turn 'what about girlfriends?'

'He talked of a French girl and I got the idea that he didn't go without and he did chat a few up when we were out some nights but he was really picky. I bet he was beating them off with a stick on the bouncer's job but if they were drunk, smoke, fat, swore, anything would put him off. He might be in France? Yeah!' Parkinson clapped his hands together and his whole face lit up as he launched into something that clearly he thought was vital to the investigation. 'You said that was the most important thing and he spoke French, I knew that, it was because he had been in France in the army.' Harper did not share the excitement but humoured him.

'Do you know where in France he had been?'

'Paris. And he skied there and I think he went to the south as well, somewhere on the coast.'

'And these were holidays?' Added Grace cajoling with her hands in a beckoning movement for more.

'Yes, he would take the train, stop off in Paris and stuff on his way skiing. It was the only foreign place he talked about.'

'Apart from the foreign places he did not talk about' mumbled Harper in a not too helpful way. Grace tried to help Mr Parkinson out.

'How about in the UK, did he have friends or family here that he would go to, favourite regions?' Parkinson shook his head through the whole question and pulled a face that resembled sadness and said 'no nothing.'

'You said "he was loaded" how did you know that?'

'I work in mortgage software and we talked about rates and products.' Harper thought *"the winter evenings must fly by"* but nodded to keep him talking 'and he told me that he bought this place outright and was mortgage free. Well! I thought he must have had an inheritance but he said that his mum and dad did leave some but he had the army pension and that he earned loads from the security work. He had a good tan, must have spent months in the Middle East. Danger money and all that.'

'So was he flash?'

'No' they all followed Parkinson's eyes as they looked about the place. It was comfortable, plain, tidy and could have been described as Spartan in that it was fitting for a fighter. 'He didn't work much so maybe he was saving it.'

'Well Mr Parkinson, we know that in the past few months this house was sold and Mr Richardson spent a considerable amount. Any idea on what?'

'You said he sold this place? Wow.' He carried the look of surprise again. Good coppers do have a magical presence of mind, maybe even second sight to see into the future. Grace and Harper were not surprised by the next dumb question, 'I didn't see a For Sale board?'

'No Mr Parkinson, he didn't have a bag with swag written on it either' thought Grace with some exasperation. They were getting nowhere and she tried to sum up with

'no I suspect he wanted to keep that a secret, as he seemed to keep so many other things. It would seem that he had no female friends, no money worries and was as nice as pie. He has stolen a large amount of money and kidnapped someone after liquidating his main asset and cleaning out his bank account. But, he may be in France, as he speaks French.'

As Grace physically slumped at the end of her summing up, Harper decided to close off the final items they needed to know. 'So did Mr Richardson have other friends that we should talk to?'

His reply was the shaking of the head and the repeated faux look of sadness.

'No, sorry.'

'And as you have been here before can you have a look round. Touch nothing. Let us know if you see anything out of place or unusual to you.' Parkinson rose and padded into the kitchen and then up the stairs after a while. Harper and Grace followed at a discreet distance looked at one another and rolled their eyes.

'So no ties, plenty of money and he could be in France as he has been there on holiday. However, now he has actually been to France and lived there he might be sick of the place.' They let Parkinson pass them as he descended the stairs. Harper muttered 'and this guy is about as useful as a turd in a chocolate box.'

'So Mr Parkinson, anything strike you?'

That face and shaky head again. Harper guided him towards the door and started on the platitudes 'well thanks for your time and if you do think of anything that you should share then call the station and pass it on.'

As Mr Parkinson stopped and shook their hands he did look back into the living room and said 'as we were talking I did think of something missing and as I walked around I wanted to check that they weren't anywhere else. It might be nothing, but his books.' He pointed and they all looked at the books, but also at the place on the shelf where there was a gap. 'His books on sailing have all gone. You did know he was in the Marines and liked sailing?'

Eighteen

Carl left the car quickly and went a little way into the vegetation that clung to a vertiginous slope. He looked downwards and moved this whole torso from left to right in a penguin like movement. Louise watched him and decided that he was making an inspection of something distant, or perhaps difficult to read. He was clearly satisfied and came quickly back to the car and opened the boot. Whilst the tail gate lifted he opened the passenger door.

'Sorry, I should have let you out first. Just grab what you can carry', he walked back to the boot and was threading his hands through the straps of a holdall and scooping a cardboard box into onto his hip 'and follow me.'

He disappeared with some pace down through the vegetation and Louise was outside and alone for the first time since she had stepped onto the bus that morning. This was the time to run. She knew there was a good distance back to the larger road and the track seemed to peter out. There was another car, a large four-by-four type parked nearby but she could see from its misted windows and dusty appearance that its owners were not nearby. There were pathways leading down hill, everything seemed to be leading down hill. Louise could see nowhere to run to so picked up the surprisingly heavy cool box and followed Carl. On leaving the road and heading downwards Lou soon saw that at the bottom of the slope was an expanse of water. She heard an engine start and looked towards the sound and saw movement and carried on downwards. The path was short but took sharp turns to relieve the descent and then led to a narrow jetty of plank and scaffolding pole. Tied to the jetty was a yacht. Lights glowed inside, she could see Carl inside busying himself with some arrangements, he was busily moving one way and another, switching things on, maybe switching things off, perhaps putting things away or getting things out. He suddenly appeared in the open rear of the boat.

'The cool box, great, we will get that into the fridge later' and he beckoned in an urgent fashion for Lou to bring it over.

'It's a boat. Is it yours?'

'Yes!' Carl stood upright and beamed at her, the proud father, 'I don't steal everything. It is mine and I will introduce you properly but the tide is going to be with us in about ten mins, which will be perfect, so we can't hang about. Can you get more of the gear please?'

He swung the cool box around and picked up the holdall that he had left on the jetty and disappeared back below, clearly busy in his work to prepare the boat. His whole demeanour had changed, she thought, as she took the three strides to travel the length of the jetty and re-enter the tree line. She was bemused by the character of the man that had forced his way, violently, into her life dragged her from that life and now seemed to beckon her into a new life. She leaned forward and placed her hand on her knees as she breathed more deeply and stepped up the incline. He so swiftly and forcibly became the controller in her life and with a gun and cheese wire could have taken her life and now he was "please" and "thank you" and they seemed to be preparing for a cruise. She stood upright, arms on her waist and stretched, put her head back and blew out a breath upon reaching the car. Surely she should run. He was clearly unstable, morphing from one character to the next, although each new character was much more pleasant than the last. She picked up a further holdall and a cardboard box and headed back. He had stormed into her life and they looked to be heading off still further from normality, continuing on this alien journey into an alien environment but since he had put that gun away there seemed to be some normality and even some predetermination in their being together. She descended with her light but bulky burden and crossed from solid ground onto the jetty. She would carry on with this voyage of discovery.

Carl stepped onto the jetty and started heading towards the car at pace 'this should be the last of it' he swivelled as he passed her and walked backwards while he talked 'just store those below and have a look about', his voice rose as he turned and started on the incline and said over his shoulder 'make yourself at home.'

She stepped aboard with some difficulty navigating over the wire railings and stanchions with her boxes. She stepped down into the cockpit, bypassed the wheel and gingerly stepped down the companionway. She liked what she saw. There was headroom and plenty of light that reflected off polished wood and light plastic. There was a galley to her left, cooker, sink and worktops that extended from the bulkhead into the centre of the boat. She could imagine washing up leaning to her right against the work surface and cupboard for some support. Forward of the kitchen was a seating area and folding table. It looked comfortable and books lined the narrow shelf behind the seats. There was a wall with a door within ahead. She walked forward toward that and negotiated the mast that pierced through the whole cabin as it headed to its footing. Bracketing the door were two nice pictures, large, framed photos of sunsets and beaches. Through the door was a cabin with a triangular shaped bed in the bows. There was room for a dressing table of sorts, drawers and cupboards. Above was a clear hatch with a complex looking locking system. It looked like it would surely keep out the worst weather, but Lou just was lost in the thought that you could lie in bed and see the stars. She turned and headed back towards the stern. Opposite the galley was a large cupboard and upon opening that door she discovered a very neatly packaged toilet, washbasin and shower room. The toilet was not built for comfort, the basin seemed to fold and the whole room was built so that it could be hosed down by the shower head jutting out from above the basin.

'Cosy', muttered Lou. Beside the shower room was a compact desk area. It reminded Lou of a niche within a monk's cell in the way it was stripped to the minimum space and furnished with one purpose. Books and electrical equipment were shelved against the exterior of the toilet wall. She could see a radio, laptop, printer and other various dials and readouts. She could see that some showed direction, perhaps depth but others were alien. A chart was spread upon the desk with pencil lines and notes.

As she ascended the steps back towards the deck she looked for a hand hold for her left hand and noticed a small curtained off section above the chart desk. If royalty were aboard it could have concealed a plaque to be drawn back with a tassel rope. As she stood on the steps she pushed the curtain away toward the hull to reveal a bed area reaching away under the deck. To try to remove some of the claustrophobia provided by sleeping on a shelf, a small window was provided.

'Compact and bijou' Lou muttered as she returned to deck. She looked about the deck and then up towards where the cars were parked. She saw Carl with the last of the bags. It seemed that the last bag was the one that she had been pushing bricks of cash into earlier that day. It was swung over his shoulder and he was adjusting or holding something with both his hands as he snaked through the woods, it could have been an animal cradled in his hands and then she got a clearer view. He was loading the handgun. She stood immobile with wide eyes and waited for the bullet.

Nineteen

They stood on the narrow pavement only one step from the door of Carl's house and had an urgent conference. Grace counted things off on her fingers at the appropriate times. 'Can you get someone on the phone to the coastguard, or is there a DVLA for boats? Find out if he has a boat, let's check with her parents if she has been sailing, oh scrub that, it won't achieve anything. Harps we need to get some bloody momentum! I will see James Munro now, I bet he is Scottish, that will top my day off. You get back to the office and get fireworks up arses. Where are their phones, any sightings of them and most of all are they Bonnie and Clyde. I will get back with you ASAP'. She stopped at this point and raised her hands towards her chest and inhaled and exhaled whilst turning her eyes upwards, she put on a show of relaxing, 'then I will brief the chief and maybe make the local news.'

James Munro was Scottish. Large and muscular but also getting some fat going there. He was wearing the standard doorman crombie, off white shirt with clip on tie and an 'I used to be in the army and never spend more than £5 on a hair cut' hair cut. He had dandruff and Grace wondered whether he would be interested in a hair consultation at Toni and Guy's. He also loved himself and had been talking more about himself than Carl and had winked at her once and that was once too often.

'Sorry Mr Munro' she closed her eyes and raised her hands in frustration and indicated that he stop, 'back to Mr Richardson, time is precious here, you made it clear that he considered and rejected the French Foreign legion so I don't need to know what your involvement, gallant as it was, was. Please keep to the point, which I think was that you have no knowledge of where in France he may be, if he is in France?'

'Aye sorry, I am a one for my tales' he winked and leaned in towards her, she fought the temptation to punch. 'No he talked of Paris and I know he was there with the Marines attached to the embassy, but' he tapped his first finger against his nose, 'he kept his duties to himself, secret squirrel.'

'Did he talk of boats and sailing?'

'No can't say he did'

'Are you sure? Never, it's important?'

He shook his head.

'Tell me about his girlfriends.'

'Well' he placed his hands on the table and leaned back, you could tell that he was going to embark on something expansive, 'this place' he looked about as he drew himself back to table 'is full of opportunities for the right fella.' Grace waited for the wink and it duly arrived, 'Carl and I' he shrugged 'you know how it is with authority figures and young girls it is like shooting fish in a barrel, or it should have been but he just was not interested. He said they were not his type and turned em down.'

'Quite the professional then, or did he have a regular girlfriend instead?'

'Well, none that I know of and I didn't think it was odd, he just made out he was right choosy. Not his type, tarty, was the way he referred to them.'

'Do you know this girl?' Grace held a picture up and saw another shake of the head, she saw a lot of that in her job.

'See loads of faces but I don't recognise her, she may have been here though, just can't rightly say.'

'Where did he get a gun?'

'Not from me!' Grace got the idea that he would not be winking for a while. She was pleased by that. She noticed that he leaned back sharply as if *she* had drawn a gun. She leaned forward, leading with her chin, narrowed her eyes, pressing an advantage; for no other reason than she could.

'You know he had a gun, with your macho swagger and bravado I bet you two couldn't bear to be without one!' she spat it out with menace.

A civvy might have raised their hands in mock surrender at that point and pleaded ignorance or delivered an elaborate lie. He took a different route as he leaned back into the table to meet her stare.

'You have Carl all wrong. He's nay like us' he pitched his thumb behind his shoulder towards the two doormen actually stood near a door '*he* played it straight', he jabbed the table, then flattened his hand and swept it across in front of himself 'whether he was in and out' (which Grace took to mean the services) 'he did it by the numbers and by the book, if you are looking for a loser', he kept his gaze fixed on her but she could see his eyes were looking for the word, 'for a psycho, or something then you have the wrong guy. Look, we may pick a fight we can win with a piss head sometimes and cop a feel with a lass that we shouldn't, but not Carl. If he got a gun then I didn't know about it.' His demeanour changed from frisky to business like. His body moved upwards as he took a breath, inspiration for inspiration. He seemed to realise that he was not chatting up a lass to cop a feel, but was being interrogated by a cop to get a feel of what this bank robber and kidnapper was about. 'Do you know the type of gun as I might be able to say what conflict it came from? Most likely Bosnia.'

'All we have is 9mm shell cases and a round that will be pulled from a ceiling.'

'Well that would be easy to break down and get back with your personal kit, or get back in the stores, we had lots of vehicles we take out and back, you could hide a 9 easy enough without risking your career. He would have taken that route, that was the guy he was, break it right down into parts, spread them over a Land Rover or two then reassemble at some time. If it was a NATO weapon then if you lost some parts it would be easy enough to get the spares without questions. He would have planned it out.' He tapped his temple 'he was a thinker and leader, he probably hated working here and taking *orders* from me. In fact I know that is true as I hated giving him orders. He was too good for this', his head descended to look at his hands, palm down on the table separated, by a ring of rheumy residue from a glass or bottle between them from the night before, or perhaps the night before that.

'So when was the last time you saw him?'

'Poofff' he blew air through pursed lips and raised his eyes skywards 'two months ago. It might have been your lot's fault he stopped' he jabbed a low finger at Grace 'he had to stay late, and we stop late enough as it is, as a girl had a bag stolen. Carl actually found it in the ladies lav, but the money, phone and stuff was gone. He had to stick about just cos your uniforms said he should. At the end of the night he's said to me that he had had enough. He was nice about it though. Just looked tired and bored with it.' He shrugged 'We said we would keep in touch and I have rung him when we are short but I haven't seen him.'

Grace sensed that this had run its course, she decided to wrap it up with a mental clear out of the little she has learnt. 'So he was not here for the money, or the enjoyment of it, maybe even hated it as he did not like the clientele or taking orders from those he used to command and then left when a drunk girl lost her purse. But he is a nice decent chap. Makes you wonder why he ever started working here and how he's ended up kidnapping and robbing banks.'

Twenty

Lou swallowed and shuddered at seeing the gun. Out of sight was out of mind and to her it was such an unfamiliar thing. He noticed her discomfort.

'Sorry, that was a bit clumsy.' He stopped in his tracks and turned the gun around in his hand so he held the barrel and proffered it towards her. 'The plan is to take you to France and drop you there. If I leave you somewhere remote then, by the time you have got inland and found someone who understands, I will have had time to get well offshore. Especially if you take your time a bit. I plan to sail on' he began to spread his hands wider 'to the Caribbean, South America, the Pacific, Asia and there' he raised the gun slightly, still holding it by the barrel 'this might be handy, some places are a bit lawless and' he delivered a Gallic shrug 'I am an outlaw, but after what has happened I think it is best if you take this now.' His hands moved in a practiced fashion and the gun came apart and she recognised he had ejected the magazine and he held out both parts to her. 'The gun is safe, take these below and put them somewhere, hide them away and you can tell me where they are when you disembark.' He stood holding them out and as he was on the jetty and she in the well of the boat he looked messianic as if his hands were pierced and not holding something seconds ago she feared. She stretched out her hands towards him, took both parts and then juggled them into her cupped hands and pulled them closer to her chest as they were heavier than she expected. He swung the last holdall, (the one with the cash within it) onto the decking. 'Can you take that below too, just put them into one of the lockers, I'll cast off'. He headed for the bow and left her to descend the companionway. She clutched the gun to herself and lowered the bag in front of herself and then placed the bag down, unzipped it and placed the gun within the money. She closed the zip firmly shutting away some things that she did not want to dwell upon. She now wanted to put the bag out of sight and she remembered caravanning with her parents and the tardis like storage required for a teenage girl on holiday. She picked a seat to kneel in front of and lifted the foam and fabric cushions and then the slatted base. She could see the steep chine of the keel. Most of the space was taken up by a folded arrangement that looked like a wind vane. She could read "Self Steer" marked on the blades but the bag fitted without many issues. She replaced everything and before getting up listened carefully. He was on the foredeck. She could hear and feel it. She also felt the boat move in a way that was unfamiliar. His footsteps went swiftly overhead and then the engine note made a step change as it engaged with the propeller. The boat moved in a purposeful way leaving the berth and land. Clearly he had been busy above and had not been sneaking a look at her hiding place. She felt some trust.

As she walked aft she looked up the companionway and saw he stood at the wheel looking all around with a concerned eye. Was he seeing if someone was watching or did he always look like that when leaving a confined channel. His sweeping eyes taking in all he commanded fell onto her and he smiled.

'First lesson', he beckoned her to come up and gestured at the wheel. He moved a lever and the engine stepped up again as she emerged into the cockpit. 'Take the wheel as I get the perishables stowed. We have loads of space and you are heading for that buoy, the green one, way off. Pass close to that with it on this side' he gestured with an outstretched arm and hand. All his fingers in line and his body turned. There was no doubt what he meant.

'Keep if on the left?'

'Yes, or to port' he exaggerated the word. 'Get a feel for it' he made a rocking movement holding an imaginary wheel, 'you will find her responsive.' And with that he was gone. She felt more trust and nerves. She did get a feel for it and recognised the responsiveness of the ship to the wheel. She aimed for the buoy in the distance and fixed the course as steady as she could. She could hear banging and rustling below and imagined things going into cupboards, into the fridge and below bunks. She looked at the buoy and re-fixed her course. More concentration required. The mooring had been remote. Maybe nothing more than a creek leading quickly into a river that shortly opened out into a bay. The closer that Lou got to the buoy the more apparent it became that a sharp right turn at that point would lead between promontories and into the open sea. The flooded valley behind them was steep banked and heavily wooded and only a few lights in the warm evening betrayed a living soul. She wondered if binoculared eyes would be able to make out their escape. She thought not as the distance between shore and them was growing quickly. She pulled the wheel again as the buoy moved away from where she intended and she could see it clearly now. The number four was painted upon it and guano streaked down its flanks. The gulls could have been trying to confuse by masking it or making it look like fourteen. She felt the breeze push against the boat and against her. Her cardy left no protection and was lifted in the wind and her skirt banged on her leg. She smelt the pine and leaf mould smell mingle with fermented seaweed. The buoy was healed well over in the pull of the outgoing tide and white water lapped about it tugging it towards the open sea like an excited child pulling a reluctant parent. She turned smartly about and headed for the open sea. The offshore wind was stronger now they were away from the lee of the land and the tide was perhaps moving more swiftly. The turn was much swifter than she expected. Carl peeked up at her.

'Heading out?'

'Yes!' she could not help but sound excited. She was surprised at the tone of her own voice, almost disembodied. Before she could stop she added 'This is great!'

'Wait till we get the sails up' he said as he emerged from below. He took a look about. 'Fabulous, keep on that course and keep an eye out for other boats as we get into more open water.' He said the last over his shoulder as he headed over the cabin roof to the foredeck. He worked on the sails, removing ties, covers and such like and then unfurled two triangles of sail. The foresail first and then the larger mainsail. She looked in awe. He moved with ease and purpose. It seemed that nothing was superfluous and everything worked as required. The sails were flapping in the wind but she could see ropes being shaken by the sails that led back towards the cockpit. She could see that these would be tightened to get them under sail. He tidied things away, looked about and under the sails to check the horizon and the shore. They were in more open water and the wind was pushing the sails and taking the heat from her body. She shivered and then gave herself a shake. She would have to find something to wear. He returned to her and she made to move away from the wheel.

'One more minute.' He ignored her offer and tightened the foresail. 'OK, head more in that direction' he made that definitive whole body pointed gesture, like a pointer dog showing the way to a fallen duck. The sail filled and pulled the boat over into a heel. Lou moved her footing.

'She is coming alive' said Carl with zeal in his voice as he cranked and wound a rope to get wind into the mail sail. The boat heeled more. It pushed against the rudder and she had to respond to maintain the course. The boat lifted and fell and Lou had to find her footing again and try to fix the boat on the heading that Carl had pointed to. He turned the engine off and she heard those silent noises that had always been there but were revealed through loosing the thrum of the engine. Spray splashed, bubbles were created and died in a hush and wind blew past her head and pulled strands of hair to strum across her ear. They smiled at each other.

'Glad you are here.' She thought it was a question, then realised that it had been a statement. She replied none the less.

'Yes, I am.' She had surprise in her voice and moved away from the wheel as he calmly took it from her.

'You must be cold and I think you will be lucky.' She moved into the gap of the companionway and wrapped her cardy about her with folded arms. 'I bought the boat recently and without seeing the guy selling it. He had an illness and I bought it via a broker with all the kit aboard. It is clear he sailed with his wife and their stuff is still here. I was trying to get it back to them but when I talked to her it was clear she had other things on her mind and I did not get around to throwing it out. Firstly, I thought they would want it, then I thought it too good to throw out and then time was against me. I know there are waterproofs, in the fore cabin and hope they fit.'

She went below and gingerly made her way through the cabin as it now seemed unfamiliar as it was canted over and moving in a leisurely heaving motion. She went into the cabin and sat on the bed remembering advice from her mother; put things down and they won't fall down. She looked in the thin wardrobe and took down a jacket and salopettes. They had bright patches and reflective stickers to show they meant business. She held the jacket up. Not her colour, but it would fit and it did look warm. Also hanging were some thermals. Not flattering. A bit 'old lady' but they would be welcome. At the bottom of the wardrobe, in a heap and at odd angles due to the slope of the keel was a pair of boots. She picked them out and subconsciously kicked off her shoes although she was not planning to put the boots on yet. She decided to look in the drawers below the mirror. The first drawer held normal accoutrements for a stay away, manicure set, sunglasses, brushes, sun cream, lip balm, some make up, pencils and pens, perfume, tampons and industrial strength moisturiser. The next drawer had socks, bikini, pants and a sole bra. She smiled, as she lifted them out it seemed strange to be going through someone else's knickers. It also seemed strange that everything else she had looked at was rugged, functional and old woman and then the briefs, well were brief. She had some similar herself. The lowest drawer had tops and shorts and some light deck shoes. She swivelled to look at the same arrangement on the other side of the door and had a brief look at Carl's clothes. Neatly folded, regimented and in order. Only the top drawer was different in his accoutrements were more male and sparing taking up less room, so a camera and tools were stowed there. She expected he would be using her moisturiser then.

She stripped down to her own bra and pants then decided to forgo the bra when she looked at the thermals. She often did that on holiday and it seemed right to do the same now. It was a constraining, freedom thing. Like clock watchers taking off their watches on holiday. She did that too. She pulled on the warmest socks she could see and then stood on the listing floor and leaned on the wardrobe to put on and adjust the salopettes. She put a lively looking top on next. She had a pick of a few and liked this one the best. It was new, an expensive brand and could see what Carl meant about not wanting to throw these things away. She had a careful look at the hair brush before using it and then slipped on the jacket and worked out the zip. It was recessed into a flap to keep the water out. She stopped to glance at herself in the small mirror. Moving about to get a view of parts that she wanted to look at. She tucked some hair away behind her ears and stepped into the boots. She was pleased with what she saw in the mirror.

The clothes could have been chosen for her.

Twenty One

Grace had picked up a coffee on the way and sat in the car sipping it with her eyes closed for a five second spell. She had been apart from Harper for eighty-six minutes but most of those were with Munro and driving. She had used the toilet at the nightclub and those moments of solitude and silence and this one were fleeting. She opened her eyes, took another sip and headed into the office.

The office was mainly open-plan, modern with nice views out to the Cotswold escarpment away in the distance, enticing the eye to look away to the horizon dotted with trees, common and exposed limestone in a few spots. The roads that did snake up and over the limestone ledge hid their rough ugliness behind trees and hedges so it brought a fine vista of unbroken countryside into their rude office. An incident board had been set up with dates, times, pictures and facts but Grace swept past that and looked for Harper. When she entered he was in a huddle of PCs and DCs and had a phone in his hand. He was looking pleased with himself.

She had asked for momentum and fireworks up arses and it would seem that Harper had delivered. He noticed her approach and put the phone down without saying anything into it.

'Just ringing you, I have some news that I think you will like.'

'Super, it is about time things started to fall into place.' She continued to walk on towards her desk, 'let me eat this' she held up a tuna and mayo sandwich, 'and you can make my day.'

'How was Munro; of any use?'

'I found it very interesting Harps' she ripped the cover from the sandwich and pulled chunks from it and popping them into her mouth. Harper did think that she ate in a peculiar way, quite posh. 'Munro was very similar to the neighbour and repeated his tale that our ruthless robber and kidnapper is nice as pie, wouldn't hurt a fly.' She settled into her chair and looked over the desk at Harper and ignored the PC, emails would be a distraction. 'I am beginning to think that this is an inside job.' She leaned forward with her elbows on the desk and gestured towards Harper with some tuna. 'I don't know what your good news is yet and I don't want to steal your glory but I think she is involved.' Harper looked interested, or was that feigned interest he crossed his arms. She brushed some crumbs away and continued. 'He didn't need the money to keep a habit going, seemed to be stable and could work if he wanted. The motive is missing. Both Munro and neighbour said he didn't have a girlfriend but from the stuff at his place it indicates that he did know her, well enough to get into her knickers.' Harper seemed pleased that she had conceded that point to him. 'So', she drew her lips back into a grimace, blew out from her nose and blinked, 'I think she put him up to it. Bored stupid at the bank and fed up of pushing other peoples' money around they hatched this plan to get their hands on as much as they could. Whatcha think?' She leaned back and the chair's springs and swivel helped her to swing into a comfy position.

'But ma'am his place is clean as a whistle, like he knew he was going away and we should go and see what hers is like for ourselves, but the PC on site says it looks like she has just popped out to the shops.'

'We will have to see her place tomorrow, but

sometimes my flat looks like laundry day at St Trinian's, and I bet you and Mrs Harper have a lovely clean house, doesn't make us bank robbers.'

I don't have your knickers in my house either thought Harper, but he knew that she was probably right. He also knew that he had to let on what he had found out. 'Well ma'am, if you think she was the brains behind it you had better have a look at what I found out.'

Harper, smiled and lent his head to one side and brought a file onto the desk. He pulled paper from the thin file as aid memoires; 'they knew each other. I looked at the only record we had on her. She reported a theft earlier this year and pulled what little we have on that crime number. She lost her handbag in a nightclub and the name jumped out as it was the club that you have just left, and the bag was found by' and they both said the name together 'Carl Richardson.'

'Good work Harper'. Grace took the offered paper from Harper but then put it onto the desk without looking at it. 'Munro just recounted the tale to me. Richardson stopped working at the club straight after. So they met that night, got chatting and bingo, hatched a robbery plot.'

'Stranger things have happened ma'am, but all we know from this is that they met. We have his statement that she reported the bag's loss, the door staff searched for it and then he searched the ladies toilets and found it there, minus its contents.'

'The start of a lovely relationship, who said romance is dead.' She popped the last morsel into her mouth and pushed more crumbs onto the floor and with some relish finished with; 'so we have her fingerprints on the glass at his house, her possessions at his house and a fixed time and place that they were together. I think we can all agree that they knew each other. Next!' She looked at Harper expectantly as he clearly had more to say.

'The phones have been recovered by West Lothian police.' Another sheet of paper was passed over and she took in the photo. 'They were found tucked into an artic at the Annandale Water services. They were both together in that plastic bag. They are off for prints. The driver's previous stop was Strensham Services where he spent an hour and that ties up with them heading straight there from the bank. A straightforward ruse to throw us off the scent. However', Harper seemed to have some happy news approaching 'we have CCTV from Strensham Services, not the best in the world but we didn't have a large time window to search and the quality is good enough to identify them and to get a licence plate. And there they are.' He handed over a picture of two people in a car 'the PNC gave us a hire company. That then led to a car within a Cheltenham branch and it was hired only this week by....' Harper's voice had been rising in triumph and he now paused for effect. *He should be on the stage* thought a hooked Grace.

'Louise Byrd'. Harper handed a hire agreement copy across the desk.

'Paid by cash, provided her driving licence, signed for it herself and drove it away.'

Twenty Two

Carl was pleased with what he saw as Louise took the wheel again. He could see the anticipation and excitement in her eyes. It had been a long day for her and that had followed a long night but she had taken the wheel like a child arriving at school for their first day at senior school.

'If I take you through a few things then I will leave you to sail her and get some food on. The wind is getting up and we will have a fine sail. There is nothing to run into and we will have light for a good few hours. All you need to do is head on this course' he pointed to a large compass held within a dome that was slightly ahead of the wheel. 'OK; lesson two.'

He took her through the points of sailing and she swung the wheel and saw the effect of the wind upon the sails, watching for the flap, slap and quivering of the foresail as the wind spilled from it. She felt the heel and speed of the boat change as its aspect to the wind changed and felt for the speed that the boat eagerly took from the wind. After each experiment Carl would provide a 'Good, now bring her back to the course' and she would move the wheel and focus on the compass card swinging to her command. He was pleased with his student and tended to the trimming of the sails explaining what he was doing as he did it. She asked questions that he readily answered and then he stood behind her shoulder looking down the length of the boat with her.

'So I think you know enough to get to France.' He quickly, almost accidentally, squeezed her shoulders. 'The forecast is for more wind but it will still be behind us so just sail as you want to with the wind. If you need to come off the course to make the most of the wind then you do it. I will be back on deck before it gets dark with some food and then you can have a sleep.'

His hand lingered on her shoulder as he moved away, extending his arm as he went to allow it to stay there for a while, then it slipped over the fabric as he went below.

She was alone again and trusted to sail with the wind as she liked. The land was still behind and over her right shoulder but it was becoming less distinct as distance and dimness built around them. Lights flickered on and the first lights she noticed were the great lights of lighthouses flashing and sweeping out from the shoreline. She could also see vessels with lights dotted around them and, as the time went on, the lights on shore became clearer than the shore itself. Red and white of cars, yellow of streets and sparkling arrays from sea-side towns.

She could see Carl dart past the companionway steps as he moved around the galley. The smell of cooking drifted up with the clattering ensemble of pot, on pan, on cooker. She could also see that he sat at the chart table between stirring the meal and made reference to the bank of electronics and checking marks on the charts. He seemed satisfied that all was well on chart and on cooker and she heard talking and laughter as the radio came on. She could not make out the words as it was not loud but she could hear the comedic pauses being filled with studio laughter and in places Carl's own chuckles added in.

Louise could see in this window Carl's happiness in the world. He was relaxed and enjoying life yet that very morning he was pointing a gun at her. Surely the extremes of anger, fear, relaxation and calmness would tear normal people apart. This abnormality in his ability to swing through all states and be able to bring terror and affection, for that is what she had felt at times, was disturbing. She fixed her course and looked at the waves about her. They were starting to crest at points and break their heads into foamy tops as the wind pulled their tips away to join the wind in flight for a while. As the sea could one day be a millpond and another a crashing morass then couldn't people also be that way? It was still the sea, he was still Carl.

He appeared on deck bearing gifts, two bowls of pasta and sauce in one hand, cutlery in his pocket and two mugs of tea.

'Hot, hot, hot' he said in an elevated way to show it was not too hot and placed the mugs onto a small, deep tray ahead of the wheel and wedged the food onto the seats. 'Let me take over and you dig in. I have assumed no sugar in your tea and if you don't like my cooking then I would be happy for you to be ship's cook.'

He stood by the wheel and held it in place with his leg for a while then wrapped a cord, that seemed to be in place for this very reason, around a spoke of the wheel to hold the course and ate with both hands.

It was nice simple al fresco fare and warming, filling and copious. Lou took up position in a place that would become familiar to her, her back on the cockpit bulkhead looking back towards the wheel and with both feet up on the bench so that she was in a warm, protected and comfortable curl, whilst looking back towards where they had been.

'Not much for pudding'. Carl pulled a cellophane wrapped packet of two cakes from his pocket and handed it across. 'Both for you' he added pulling out another that he delicately pulled open for himself.

'I hope you have plenty of food' said Louise letting loose a few crumbs to fall to the wet deck.

'Loads actually. We will both get through the fresh stuff quickly but I stocked up for a long voyage and the previous owners left plenty of tinned. Even with two of us we will be fine for a while and we can get more in France.'

'So what is the plan?'

'Well, first things first, you get some sleep. The plan was, with this wind, for me to make a night crossing and sail along the French coast all day tomorrow and then put into port tomorrow. If it is OK with you then I will keep you until the following day? I can stock up a bit, take on water then sail down the coast a little and let you get onshore somewhere remote at night fall. If you take a sleeping bag and blankets and spend the night ashore then hand yourself in I would expect that I can get well clear and into the shipping lanes enough to get away again. You would still have the money to hide as before.'

'And what will you do then?'

'Sail on.' Carl paused and took a gulp of tea. 'She' he nodded at the boat 'can take me anywhere I want and as long as I am careful to avoid US customs and UK territory for a good few years then I think I can sail the world.'

'Won't you miss England?'

'I expect I will, but I have lived abroad in a few countries and feel the enjoyment of returning to those countries in the same way that I enjoy returning to England. I think you enjoy returning as for most people it is a stopping place. You leave, you travel, you do things' his body began to sway in rhythm to what he was saying 'you see the sites, you spend your time doing things, doing the things you travel for and then you come home and stop doing them. You come home and relax, which for most people is the reason they actually left UK; they leave as they want to relax, but then don't do that until they get back. And when they get back they say, "I am glad to be back and now I can relax". Daft really, so as long as I travel and keep enjoying it then I won't want to get back to the UK.'

'Don't you have family?'

'Only a brother in Australia. I might turn up on his porch one day for a laugh; his wife is a lawyer and she will crap herself.' They both laughed 'this whole escapade will be worth it just to see her face. She will round up the children and take them off in case I pass on the black sheep gene of the family through osmosis. He will be cool with it all though as he knows.' He seemed to have taken the conversation to a point that he had not meant to. He stopped and looked at the wind and sails and adjusted course a wee bit that made no difference to anything. Louise prompted him.

'He knows what?'

She did not fill the pause, she waited and eventually, Carl continued.

'He was in the forces too. You have to be in to know how it feels. It is an exclusive club at times.' He looked off to the horizon. 'He is an older brother and I followed him in, our parents died far too young and after school it was the best place to go to keep a semblance of family. The army provides that. But it teaches you to kill and compartmentalise, to inflict pain and aid in equal measures, but it is not great at teaching you how to discern who to hurt and who to help. Your enemy and friends are interchangeable from one day to the next. Only the army and your mates are constant. And the memories I suppose.' He shrugged at that, paused a beat then went on, 'you try to leave the bad experiences behind, in Bosnia, the Gulf and other backstreets around the world but they follow some of us about like a mongrel dog. He knows that and he got away through promotion, emigration and marriage. I joke about his wife but she anchored him.' His focus turned to look down into Louise's eyes, 'she saved him through love, providing a family and getting him physically away from the triggers to his memories and he told me that "I should do the same and go to him". He was right. I got more and more embroiled with the forces when I left. I could not let go. I said that it was for financial reasons and they were', his hands tightened on the wheel and his movements were more forceful for a second then it relaxed and he let whatever memory he was replaying to move off. 'Being a soldier for hire was lucrative and we kept some of the camaraderie but we lost the esprit de corps and discipline and spent a lot of time watching our own backs and protecting guys and companies earning much more than we ever would. And they were taking money from the people and places that needed it most. In the army you follow orders, there we followed the money. So I got out, and he was pleased with that. But I am not a great one for sitting about so travelling and sailing were what I wanted to do and so I planned for this' he swept his hand over his domain, it was all his to the horizon, 'but I needed more funds than I had and so I took it. I know that is wrong but when you have seen pallet loads of US dollars delivered to a warzone alongside ammunition, taking the space on a plane that medicine, or doctors could have taken then the worth of money changes. I am sure you have been told that you can achieve anything. It isn't true, it is a parental platitude. What they mean is that with the right amount of force you can achieve anything. I could force the bank' he paused and looked disconsolate and his gaze fell to the deck and he took a breath and swallowed, 'I could force *you* to give me what I wanted. That was wrong but I am not sorry. I spent years in the forces and now I am looking at years of not being in the forces. The two don't marry up for me. I left one thing, the army, but could not join the other, civilian life. So I am here between two worlds making one for myself. I am with you and I know I have dragged you into my world and I am sorry for that.'

He continued to look sad but his gaze did not settle on her for a while, it went to the sails, the burgee, the sea and then to her. He saw that she was curled up, cupping her mug of tea and smiling at him.

'It's OK. It's turning into a real bank holiday adventure. Not what I expected this morning. You have frightened me, I did think you would hurt me, but I don't feel that now.'

'You look worn out Lou. Why don't you take the foreword cabin as your own and get some sleep. I will sail through the night and you can take over when you wake up. I had not banked on having a crew but I am really glad to have you here.'

She stood and said good night and headed below, taking the dirty dishes with her. She washed and rinsed the crockery and pans and took a final look onto deck. There was light in the sky and Carl was framed in the companionway with a few stars shining over his shoulders. He had pulled on hat and gloves and was stood in a steady stance looking ready for the night ahead. He noticed her looking up and raised a hand.

'Get off to bed and turn the lights out as you go through. Sleep well.'

She waved back and trudged towards the bow, got the wet-weather gear off and then stepped into the toilet. She was slightly puzzled but then pleased to see that Carl had left a new toothbrush out for her.

Twenty Three

Grace had known the Chief Constable for years. Her dad had served with him and had liked him. Her father had helped his career and she sometimes wondered how much the favour had been returned. He had also been coming to the house for years with his own wife and then with his children and Grace had only recently stopped calling him Uncle James. She had told Harper of the family connection and he was not impressed. She had mentioned it in passing when telling an anecdote about dinner parties and regretted it straight away. She wouldn't stand for a whiff of privilege or the old school tie crap getting in the way of her progression through hard work and professionalism. However, she could not help knowing that when other DCI's went up stairs to see the chief they climbed with a heavy heart and tread but she was off to see Uncle Jim. She cleared that thought from her head, just in case at some dozy moment she actually called him that in a meeting. Bit like calling your school teacher Dad by mistake.

She and Harper strode past the empty secretary's desk, for the hour was getting late, and through the open door into the CC's office. He was sat comparing a sheet of paper to the PC screen as they walked in.

'Excellent timing. If we are going to get on the ten o'clock news we had better get the story straight' he stood and waived to an area with couches, 'do we need Emily?'

'No sir. I will take you through the developments but I don't think a press release and public appeal is going to be required.'

'How so?' Grace deferred to Harper with a nod.

No point having a dog and barking yourself and she wanted Harper to shine, she liked him and wanted to help his career and face time with the CC would only help. Harper may have thought that she had no need to impress him; her career path was assured. Whatever he may have thought Grace watched her junior recount the evidence and theory with some pride.

'…and we are therefore, currently, holding a position that Louise Byrd and Carl Richardson were known to one another and are accomplices in the crime.'

The chief paraphrased to show his comprehension 'so an inside job, she the brain and him the brawn.'

'And a public appeal with the parents for her release or comments about ransom demands would not sit well with me sir' added Grace to show that she was thinking strategically. 'We have not told them as yet, thought we would talk to you first sir.'

'Thanks Grace, you don't think that the appeal would help identify where they could now be?'

'Possibly sir, we know they initially headed north on the M5 but doubled back and sent the phone decoy north. We know he can sail but we really don't know where he could be. More likely, on the balance of possibilities he is on dry ground. It is unlikely that an appeal on local news would help after this timeframe.' The chief stood up.

'Well the good news on that front is that we can get off home and resume in the morning.' He headed to his desk but continued to talk as he filed, locked and put things into bags 'so all ports and airports on lookout, licence recognition looking for the car and without worries on kidnap and ransom it becomes a waiting game to find out where they are. How much friend and family have you talked to?'

'There's not many to talk to but we will continue with that.' Harper then helpfully added to Grace's comment 'and now that we believe that they are complicit Louise's friends will be questioned again sir.'

'Excellent work; so far. Will you talk to the parents now?' The question was directed at and answered by Grace.

'Of course sir, I will do it now.' The chief gathered the last of his things and the three of them headed out closing doors and turning off lights.

'Well I know that you will be tactful with it, but be careful Grace. They won't be happy to hear that their daughter is implicated in a bank robbery.' He stopped for a second at the external doors as they were about to head in different directions but the pause also added to the emphasis on what he said next 'and this is day-one. It seems to me that you are not sure she is the brains of this outfit. Play your cards close to your chest. They were expecting a public appeal with tears and wailing. If you tell them that's not required because she is up to her neck in this, then you had better not change your mind tomorrow.'

Twenty Four

Carl was used to sailing solo and to sailing this type of boat. He was relishing this. The wind had got up more and that was fine. He had hauled down the radar deflector at midnight and stowed it away. He hoped that anyone tracing the faint reflection would simply no longer see them. He also changed course at the same time to head further south. He'd had no way to find out how closely these things were tracked or if the police could track these things. If they did then a radar trace would show a good course for Eire or the US at a push, but not a great course for where he was actually intended to go. He did not think they would trace the yacht, it was not registered to him, it was too small to be officially registered and tagged with an electronic MSSI number. As long as he got over the horizon of land radar and the RAF and Navy did not get involved than he might get away with it. He knew that lots of thicker crooks got away with it. He was as confident as his planning allowed him to be, he had done it once, done it big and got away.

He looked around the horizon which was discernable through the light of the moon, stars and sun's penumbra. The darkest part of the night had passed and dawn was approaching. He poured coffee from a thermos, locked the wheel and ducked below to check position, mark the chart and check the weather.

He made a decision then that was not rash but he would later regret. The weather continued to show a favourable and strengthening wind. Not a bad thing but Carl, looking at the chart decided to cut further towards the shore than he might otherwise have done. He wanted to turn south but staying more north within the English

Channel and in deeper waters would have been better. Had Carl thought of his unfamiliarity with his little boat in heavy seas a better decision may have followed.

He did not dally below and got back on deck, released the wheel moved more southward, trimmed the sail and watched a beautiful dawn that belonged to him alone.

Twenty Five

Grace was offered the armchair and Mr and Mrs Byrd took up the sofa. All of them leaned forward and Grace replayed the speech she had prepared on the way to see them. An officer stood in the background looking like she was taking notes and preparing a handbook on how not to break bad news.

'My team have been working hard today and we know who took part in the robbery today. We know his name is Carl Richardson and he lives here in Cheltenham. His details have been widely circulated and I am sure we will find him. Mr and Mrs Byrd, we do not think that he intended to kidnap your daughter. We do not think that he intends to harm your daughter. The reason we think that is because we have established that he knew her. He worked at a nightclub that your daughter frequented and a glass with her prints, her fingerprints on was at his house.' Mr Byrd stopped leaning forward. He straightened up, but not as if to stand, just to enable his centre of gravity to change so that he could flop back into the sofa. Mrs Byrd was slower on the uptake 'and we found items belonging to Louise at his home. We know that they could not have been taken there after the robbery. She has been to his house. So this is good news in that it is likely that she is safe and well. We just need to find out where they both are. Would you have any ideas where she may go?'

Mrs Byrd was still working to catch up, she was looking for stairs in a bungalow. 'Where he has taken her you mean?' She looked back at her husband in confusion. 'We wouldn't know where he would take her.'

'No love.' Mr Byrd struggled back upright so that he could look his wife in the eye 'she is saying that

Louise has gone with the guy 'cos she knows who he is. She's not been taken. She has gone with him. That is right isn't it, that's what the police think?' He looked dejectedly at Grace.

'It is a theory that we are working on yes but it is early days in the investigation. I would want to keep working on the clues and leads and we have many, many officers looking for them both as we speak so it is a matter of time before we find them.'

'But you don't think she has been kidnapped' stated Mr Byrd. Grace let go the last fact to convince them.

'The get away vehicle was hired by your daughter so we do not believe she was kidnapped.' The parents looked bemused. It was a look that Grace had seen a few times that day. She could not gain any more and so made a quick exit with promises to be back tomorrow and she took the policewoman to one side and asked her to wait till morning and then enquire where Louise may have gone. They might need the night to let the thought sink in that their little girl was the brains behind an armed bank robbery.

Twenty Six

Louise woke with a start. So many things were strange, the smell of salt water, the feeling of dampness, the curious firmness of the bed, the movement of the ship, the realisation that she had survived a day in captivity. However, with the last thought she simply adjusted her position in bed slightly and thought about getting back to sleep. There was a watery light through the glass hatch above her head and she could feel through the motion and evidence of spray that there was more liveliness from the boat now. She wanted to get on deck and survey the scene so she pushed down the covers and swung her feet off the bunk. There was not much choice in the wardrobe department but she took a clean pair of pants and covered herself up enough to make her way to the bathroom and there washed, changed into deck gear and headed on deck.

It was almost as if Carl had not moved. Still steady with legs set against the heel of the deck behind the wheel. The deck was heeling more than yesterday the lee gunwale was running in the higher waves and he was looking decidedly more damp. He had not lost any joie de vivre though.

'Hey, sleepy head, good morning! I have decided that you are going to make an excellent sailor. Not because you have a feel for the boat, not because you know how to read the waves, but because you can sleep at the drop of a hat. That is an important gift. Equally important is being able to make a good cup of tea.'

'Aye, aye captain.' Lou saluted and with her hand to her forehead turned back towards the companionway. She had a good look about and instinctively checked on the clock affixed to the bulkhead what the time was. The sky's darkness inferred an earlier hour than it was. The brightness of the previous day was yet to appear. The clouds and sky were more gloomy and the sea absorbed that colour into its grey depths. To add colour and lightness the sea itself broke its surface and shook free white flecks of foam that were pulled by the wind into streaks that raced away from the crests of the waves. The wind that held their course and sped them on their way was continuing to increase and push them further and faster. Nothing was within their universe apart from the sea and sky. No land. No ship. No creature.

She asked Carl about breakfast and got the kettle on and toast under way and looked at the chart whilst waiting for the whistle and browning. A clear line showed their course. It linked crosses that curved from the land into the open ocean. At each cross was a time and another number that Lou could tell from the increments were miles. She collected up the tea and toast and headed onto the deck again.

Carl curled up the toast into a mouthful and stuffed it rather unceremoniously into his mouth and after ruminating with some enjoyment he said 'you slept like a log.'

'I think it is more to do with only having four hour's sleep in forty two hours. I had a bit of a late night the-night-before-last.'

'Well I have noticed that you are late to work on Fridays.'

'You were watching me?'

'Don't flatter yourself love, I was watching the bank to see the routine on Fridays and part of the routine was you being late.'

'How often did you watch?'

'I saw you on three Fridays. From three positions at different times of the day and I came in to deposit and withdraw a few times before making the final withdrawal.'

'Did I serve you?'

'No. It was the old grumpy cow twice. And that was a disappointment as I would have preferred you to serve me.'

'Really.' She thought he was getting flirty, 'and why was that?'

'Well I wanted to see you up close but I had already laid out the plan to enter the back of the branch with you so thought that too much interaction may be a bad thing.' She thought he was not flirting. 'And I was intrigued by you.' Louise's flirtometer picked up that standard from the Leslie Phillips book of charm. She let him continue 'I wanted to know why you were late on Fridays.'

'I am late on other days too.' She let that hang then explained 'but I go clubbing on Thursdays. It is a bit of a tradition and I expect being late on a Friday is too.'

'Well it gave me an opening. A staff member to follow in and use to get into the back office.'

'So you are just using me.' She asked that in a cheeky way and took a swig of tea to try to conceal the urgency in asking the question.

'Take the wheel.' Carl pointed out the course and then he moved in front of the wheel and there they stood. Face to face, straight towards each other and in close proximity but separated by the wheel, binnacle and cups of tea. Within that strange tabernacle they were intimate but separate. He wiped his face and took a stretch.

'I was just using you to get the bank's money.' He was looking serious 'and then I used you as a hostage to get away. It is as mercenary as many of the other acts within my life. I am sorry for treating you that way. But sorry is a crap platitude. It is only slightly above "I was only joking" and means very little. All I can do is make up for what I did. I treated you as a pawn in my game and now I am treating you as guest on my boat and a fellow sailor.' He held out his hand to shake and she took it and they both seemed happy to let the hand shake move into a hand hold. She looked closely at him, at his gentle smile and his inquisitive eyes. She saw some feeling that she had not seen from him before, it could have been paternal and it was that look that triggered her to say something that was almost in reflex.

'Are you sure we've not met before?'

'No, never' was the certain reply.

Twenty Seven

Grace slept uneasily. She had gone back to her flat and reheated a prepared meal from her freezer. She vaguely remembered cooking batches of something and sealing up Tupperware pots for another day and whilst she waited for the mystery meal to cook she had the radio on and tidied up. She inspected the beef casserole with some recognition after the microwave beeped and then switched the radio off and TV on so that the homely noise continued. As the meal cooled from surface of the sun to merely volcanic she peeled off all her clothes and put on her non sexy, relaxing dressing gown. Finally, she curled onto the sofa, cradled the casserole in a tea towel and ate. The TV was making a noise but she was too tired and her brain too full to take that in. A thought was persistently drumming on her temple. It was reminding her of a basic tenet of investigation. It was a small nagging doubt that had grown into a full grown, ex-wife, low on alimony, hating the new woman in her ex-husband's life, nagging doubt. The doubt was the motive. What was the motive for an armed bank robbery when you had a healthy bank balance a pension income and someone on the inside at the bank? Some things fitted too well and others did not fit at all. Grace turned the television off and put the melted casserole container into the bin, (which would save on washing up) and headed to the bathroom and then bedroom. Before she climbed into bed she wanted to check on something. To look at something and then perhaps to sleep on it. She opened her own bedside cabinet drawer. She looked at the melange of items that were deposited. The jetsam of the bedroom seemed to be gathered there. Some of it was useful and regularly used, the manicure set for example and others items seemed to be keepsakes, that key ring in the shape of a bear, a decade old tube of hydrocortisone. It was all there in a nice, useful drawer way. Ordered chaos. Grace slid the drawer closed, rolled into the duvet and lay for a while looking at the bedside light thinking of bedside cabinets, motives and the task list for tomorrow. She looked at the light again and then switched off.

Twenty Eight

Carl loved this time the most. He planned meticulously, but there were many areas that were outside of his control. There were many variables that impacted the plan and the critical path. His expectations and innate optimism were impediments to good planning as he had tended to hope for the best, to ride his luck on occasions, to go with the flow. Sometimes that worked in his favour, but he recognised that a team would willingly, even enthusiastically, follow a well structured plan delivered by a trusted advisor but most people would be wary of a trail beset with chance and guesses. He had hoped that Louise would want to help him sail and perhaps like to learn something of sailing, but here he was with an enthusiastic and competent pupil, filled with curiosity and wonder, excitedly taking in new facts and learning new skills, asking intelligent questions and being able to take control of situations and decide things for herself after the shortest tuition. They had spent time eating breakfast and looking at the charts together and she was full of questions and he was full of answers. He loved the pupil-teacher, novice-master, relationship they had. He was proud of his new charge and they stood together in the cockpit, Lou on the wheel and Carl handing over a fresh cup of tea and ginger biscuits that he had rustled up. He looked at the compass card, then up at the setting of the sail, took a sweep of the horizon and then came back to the compass card. He could not stop himself from looking closely at Louise and feeling pride in what he had achieved. He would not change a thing. The course was correct and steady, the sails were trimmed beautifully and she looked stunning in this light with the wind lifting strands of her hair up and flying them like a burgee towards him. He put out a hand to steady himself, perhaps he would change one thing, the sea was getting choppy. He looked about the horizon again. There was a smudge of land off to their port. France was in the distance. The boat took a dip as it tipped into the trough of a wave. It picked up speed as it surfed down the face of the wave and the bow caused a splash of spray to leap as it hit the oncoming wave, jolting the deck and sending a roll of water along the scuppers.

'You told me that there was a forecast for a moderate sea state, is this moderate?'

'No' laughed Carl, 'that was a bit bumpy, it certainly looks a bit choppy ahead, let me just check something.' Carl looked towards the coast and squinted. There was a mist or haze obscuring any detail being revealed and that also meant that he could not judge how far away the coast was. Perhaps they had come too close in shore. His choice of course was one for speed. He wanted to cut the corner on Brittany and head south as soon as he could. Perhaps he had been too adventurous and led them into shallows where the tide, currents and wind could cause larger waves. He headed below to check the position and charts. He took his tea and descended the stairs single handed. They surfed another wave and he braced for the jolt as the bow pushed into the oncoming wave. The jolt was heavier and the crockery and cutlery let out a tinkle and chatter. He took in the GPS location and plotted that on the chart, marking on it their position and current time. The tide had moved them closer to the shore and onto shallower waters. Ahead of them was an even shallower area and the falling tide and wind was heaping up the waves. It would be short lived as they would sail over that and into deeper water.

'I think we are closer to the shore than I thought, if we head out into deeper water it will settle down.' This was said over his shoulder and he heard a steady 'OK' from above.

Carl turned to the companionway, steadied himself and took a swig of tea and headed up.

He had had a sleepless night, perhaps that was the cause? Was he distracted by teaching Louise about calculating depth of tide? Perhaps he should simply have put his tea down. Perhaps it was all these things coming together. Carl nearly got to the cockpit but as he raised his foot to gain that step he felt his foot rise further than he needed. The boat surfed down another wave, but this was larger, steeper. As the bow of the boat dived down and the stern lifted up it tipped Carl backwards. He watched his foot rise further and further he darted forward with his free hand but gained no purchase as the boat and his body were moving in opposite directions. He fell backwards through the companionway into the saloon of the boat. The whole boat accelerated down the face of the wave, racing with Carl to see which would hit their nemesis first. The boat won and pushed into a green wave sending a halting shudder through the ship and as the boat decelerated sharply the back of Carl's head hit the cupboard top and also decelerated sharply. There is a good blood supply to the thin layer of skin covering the skull so a small cut can bleed a lot. Large cuts also bleed a lot. Carl hit the deck and saw the hot tea cascade over himself. Only Louise saw the splash of blood. Then Carl stopped feeling much as he blacked out. His final thought was, 'this isn't part of the plan.'

Kevin Dinwoodie

Twenty Nine

The first appointment of the day had been set for an early time that Harper had readily agreed to. Grace knew that he was diligent and hardworking and she made sure that he knew that she knew, but she also pulled his leg that he needed to start the working day early as his brain worked more slowly than hers. They both knew that there was a nugget of truth in that too. She had had a good breakfast at home and had picked up two coffees and she felt and looked great. As she emerged from her car and walked up the short drive towards Louise's flat she could tell that Harper was pleased to see her, perhaps she had too many buttons undone on this blouse.

'You look pleased to see me.'

'Always pleased to see you ma'am.'

'Hmm, not sure that is actually true but have your coffee anyway. Why are you grinning, did the current Mrs Harper allow you to have a cuddle this morning?'

'Funny you mention that ma'am, but the wife was very' he pursed his lips and looked up to his left looking for the correct word *'informative* last night, she and I had a discussion about ladies' underwear.'

'Whatever floats your boat Harps, if you think oral sex means talking about it then I am not going to contradict you; but I suspect you were talking about Louise Byrd's pants. I was thinking about those too.'

'Were you thinking that things were not adding up ma'am?'

'Unfortunately' she waved to the PC on the door and went up the Cotswold stone steps, 'I was. The lack of motive bothers me' she moved through the dark hallway with its overflowing pigeon holes of post that indicated the large number of flats in the building that had transient dwellers. 'If he has access to Louise as an accomplice why fake the kidnap; and his finances are in better shape than yours and mine. He could be a greedy arse, angry at the world and trying to get back what he thinks he is owed, but you don't get that message from the people who know him.' They had ascended the fine stairs that implied the grandeur of the original house, before a property developer with stud walls and a profit margin had arrived. 'He is a tidy, guy with a tidy mind. He likes order. We can see that in his house, even down to the contents of his' she paused and used her fingers to make a parenthesis around the next word she said 'girlfriend's knicker drawer at his house. My own is a bit of a mess. It will be interesting to see what hers is like.' They had arrived at the door and Harper provided a key and they stepped inside.

It wasn't a bomb site. The flat had a good feel of informality and they both appraised the flat as they moved from room to room then settled down to have a closer look. Even small flats on this road are expensive and this had some space and two bedrooms. One was actually used and the other had a single bed but seemed to be used for storage and held a large book case. There were banking text books and other reference books, but the room was not a study. They got the feeling that the door to the room was seldom opened. The kitchen was small and held a copious amount of washing up. It was piled neatly in the sink and drainer. Harper had a good look to see if he could tell if these were meals for two, gave up and headed for the bin. To his disappointment there was little in it. Perhaps bin day had recently passed. He pushed around plastic wrappers, yoghurt cartons, receipts and other banal detritus before moving to the living room.

The matching chairs were IKEA and faced the TV'. Magazines and books sat on an older coffee table with another plate. Clearly a quick meal for one in this case. In a final sweep Harper summed it up. Much better than student digs, but the carpet was a stranger to a hoover and Mr Sheen was not a regular caller. He contrasted it to Carl's clean and tidy order. She was buying furniture and decorating as funds allowed. It would be a great flat in a few years. He didn't get the idea that she had left with the intention of never coming back. He pondered that as he sought Grace out.

'I guess they spent time at his house' offered Harper as he walked into the main bedroom. This room had been recently decorated, had matching furniture but the bed was unmade and clothes were hung on the bedstead and on a nice chair beside the dressing table. The windows made this room. That type of window that led you to walk up and look outside as soon as you entered a room. Large Georgian windows in this case looking out over plane trees and the wide Landsdown Road. It was a nice room and looked to be where Lou spent a good deal of her time when in the flat.

"Well, it isn't too bad. I get that she is a busy girl with more things on her mind than washing up and cleaning. My place looks like this during busy weeks.'

'I thought you had a cleaner ma'am?'

Grace frowned. 'My place looks like this during busy weeks *before* the cleaner comes around. It does look like the bed is only slept in by one person and there is nothing male about the place.' Grace pointed to the bedside table. 'This is as messy as mine and no order to the items.' She rummaged through the drawer. 'Not as tidy and regimented as the items at Carl's place'.

'As if he had placed them there ma'am. Isn't it more likely that he just tidied her things in the same way as he tidied his own?'

'I just feel uneasy about something, if they were in a relationship then they kept it quiet.'

'Ma'am. They knew each other from their meeting in the club. We have her prints and belongings at his house. At some point one of them had an idea', Harper sat beside Grace on the bed at this point, 'to commit the robbery. Who had the idea we don't know, what form it took initially we don't know. Perhaps', he suddenly warmed to his theory and the pace of his delivery picked up, 'she had proposed the idea of an inside job and had planned it without his participation, the usual white collar crime, a little here a little there, so it was her idea but then he put a twist on it. The inside job that looked like a robbery. It wouldn't have been the first time.'

He and Grace looked at one another as they sat on the edge of the bed. A memory of a teenage romance ran through Grace's head and she pushed the memory away.

'Well if they were going out she kept the crappy pants at his house.' Grace turned back to the knicker drawer. 'She had a right pair of granny pants at his place. I am glad to see that the girl actually had some taste'. Grace held up a matching set of lingerie and looked at the labels. 'I quite like these.'

'And that is what the current Mrs Harper and I were discussing last night.'

Grace laughed. 'Was that out loud, sorry Harps, I am sure that Mrs Harper can provide some insight on the case, what are her thoughts on this?'

'Well' he folded his arm but continued to expand his ideas and lay them out despite the gesture. 'I saw her personal things at his house as confirmation of this as an inside job but wanted to check something with Mrs Harper and so I chatted to her about the day.' Grace turned to face him fully and the teenage remembrance seemed to come back to her.

'You gave her a debrief?' He smiled and squirmed.

'No that was later ma'am.' She smiled and squirmed.

'Sorry to interrupt keep going.'

'Well the misses just asked about the pants we found at his house, how many pairs and what they were like.'

Grace thought for a second with a wrinkled brow. 'One pair; and I would say they were just on the period side of her normal day wear.' Harper offered a raised eyebrow and a head inclination to show that he wanted more explanation but did not want to actually say anything out loud at the moment. 'Not sure where you are going with this but looking at the knicker here she seems like a young girl on the pull, different to those at his flat.'

'Let's assume they are her pants, they are in a drawer with her possessions. I think that between us ma'am we can agree that they are not,' Harper seemed to be a bit flustered at this point, 'sexy, or not like the ones that are here. And that demonstrates that they have a mature relationship, he has known her for a while, she doesn't need to wear sexy underwear all the time.'

'Hang on Harper' she shook her head slowly. 'Just because she sometimes wears the same pants as your wife it doesn't mean they are in this together. If they wanted to throw us off the scent then he could have hidden their relationship'

'I think they really have been hiding their partnership and have been planning this meticulously for some time. That gives us a problem though as they did not hide her things. They seem not to care, they are so sure that we will not be able to find them. Wherever the two of them have planned to go, they think they are safe there.'

'It seems that you, Mrs Harper and I all agree something needs to be cleared up here, I just am wary of this theory that she is as involved as you think.' She rolled her eyes and pulled a playful expression. He smiled and thought he really should get off the bed as Grace had been sat holding sexy underwear, had too many buttons undone on that blouse and was looking rather lovely during their intense discussion. He stood and talked at the same time.

'Not sure why ma'am. They met, she has been to his place, has her things there and best of all she hired the get away car.'

Grace put the drawers and contents back in place 'And that is our next stop. Do they have CCTV?'

'Yes they do ma'am' he liked it when they were on the same wavelength and he was about to like it more.

'When do they open?'

'I asked the manager to get there early and have the tape cued up for us by 8.30.'

'Just time to get another coffee then. Good work Harper.'

<u>Thirty</u>

Nothing in life stays the same. Everything changes. Time passes, our experience grows colouring our future. Every single day we may travel along a routine filled with regularity, of steady practice, with metronomic expectation but every step is unique nothing is the same. However, there are times, occasionally, when it is right to say that something happens, within that background of everything being unique, that we face something that we have never experienced before.

Louise looked down the companionway at Carl. As he had fallen into the galley cupboard he had been forced to slump against it and now lay with one foot elevated on the stairway so that she could see the worn sole of his boot and the other was away facing toward the cooker. If his legs looked balletic his torso countered by being crumpled. His all-weather gear, being rucked up, puffed up like a sail due to him being forced into a forward crouch by the stairs and the cupboard. He would have looked uncomfortable but peaceful apart from the blood. There was a splatter on the worktop and a smear that proved, like a line on a chart, his route from consciousness down the cupboard to the floor and now she could see more blood running along his hair, gathering for effect, growing in size and then dripping to the floor.

She wanted to go to him but resisted and forced herself to calm down. Took deeper breaths and in a few seconds she chose a course that would change her life.

'Get a grip girl, you can do this.' She flexed her hands on the wheel and looked about wildly 'Safety first, get the boat safe and get into deeper water.' She knew the wind direction and moved the wheel, held it in place with her thigh whilst working the mainsail sheet to adjust. 'Don't worry about the course, just get deeper', she raised her voice and talked to Carl, feeling that a shout would get through his bleeding slumber 'Carl! Hang on while I get out of this swell. I am heading out like you said! I will be there soon!'

She took a look at the depth gauge and braced as the new course took them across the face of the waves and the boat rolled, pitched and heaved. 'Head wounds bleed a lot, it's what they do' she said reassuringly to herself. 'They look worse than they are, sometimes. Remember Toby at school. That was a great crack on the head, blood everywhere. One stitch. Hardly worth the bother. Calm down Lou.' She was burbling and was losing focus. She forced herself to get control of her breathing and calmed down. The depth gauge was clicking upwards although the boat continued to leap under her feet. She studied the water and could see where the water was being forced up from the English Channel by the rocks below them and where the deeper water flowed more steadily. She headed towards that and worked on the sails she did not need speed, she needed headway and a steady course and she set the sails for that. The penultimate act was to look about and no other boat was in sight. She then lashed the wheel in place to maintain that course and headed below.

She picked a moment when the boat was most steady and gingerly hopped over his leg, missed the last two treads on the stair by stepping onto the seat by the chart table and was beside him.

'You wouldn't thank me for standing on you and breaking your leg.' No response. 'What have you done to yourself.' She nearly cried but walked away and grabbed the towel from the toilet, returned to him and knelt down.

She balled the towel and pulled him from his crumpled crouch towards the passage way leading for'ard, the towel placed under his head. She tugged on his harness and dragged him down the boat. His legs and feet followed and with the right timing and force he was soon laying flat. In the confines of the small floor space she was able to roll him into the recovery position. She had a good look at the wound. There was a mass of congealed blood. She dabbed at it with the towel and achieved nothing and learnt nothing.

'Well your brains haven't fallen out.' She pulled a cushion and blanket down and covered him. As she did so she momentarily covered his face as you would a corpse. She suddenly uncovered his face and gasped with the realisation that he may be dead. She pushed her hand into his jacket and held his neck and felt a pulse. 'Stupid cow, corpses don't bleed.' She chastised herself for the momentary lapse in judgement and for feeling so much for him. What did she care if her kidnapper died? She sat on the side bunk and looked down on him. He was no longer crumpled, he just looked peaceful and sleeping now that his blood had died back to a dark stain on his dark hair. She brought her fore and index finger up to her mouth and kissed them, then placed them onto his temple. She passed a kiss along like her own father had. She smiled down on him and she shared his peace for a second or two.

She then looked up at the radio. On its front were the May Day and Pan Pan instructions. Carl had taught her the difference and what to do. She continued to stare at them. She could call for help and save his life. A life behind bars. Or she could wait for him to wake up, *if* he woke up. If he did die then what? Would she be in trouble for letting him die? Would she be in trouble for letting him live! She looked at Carl and then back at the radio. She was on a boat in the English Channel with an armed robber, with a kidnapper who was now at her mercy. A man that could actually be merciless. She saw the power that she had at her disposal to command his life. She did not consider the command that she had on her own.

'If he lives, he lives. I don't have the power over life or death.' She stroked his hair that had no blood in. 'Carl? Wake up when you are ready. I am going to head on down south.' Then as an afterthought 'don't sleep too long.' She passed on a kiss again and then headed back to adjust the course and to sail on single handed.

<u>Thirty One</u>

Grace knew what was going to happen. As Harper had talked to the manager to arrange the meeting, had walked in first and led the introduction, the manager assumed Harper was her boss. It happened with some regularity. It shouldn't get on her tits, but it did. He was good at his job and she was good at hers. She worked hard to be where she was and that included working hard at university and at getting into the force. That application process, that form, that interview she had grafted and crafted at every stage. Did anyone else submit their letter and application on heavy grade stationary, hand delivered. OK so her dad was in the force, but that meant she had to work even harder to live up to his expectations. She couldn't let him down.

So here they were running up to a dénouement. One chair to sit on that the 'manager' (barely old enough to drive himself and clearly only the manager as he was the one in the office who could spell *manager*) had waved Harper to sit on. She stood as they sat looking across the desk at one another and were entering into a preamble of pleasantries. She didn't want Harper to stand and force him to defer to her and to belittle him so she took another tack. Grace walked past Harper and stood beside the manager. He swivelled in his chair and looked up as his personal space was invaded. English lessons with Miss Price registered in his mind. He would have had a school boy erection if he was not suddenly a bit scared. She glared at him and he wheeled back slightly and leaned back slightly. She leaned forward slightly and his eyes darted at her face and cleavage.

'I am not standing up at the back of the room

listening to you guys chatting about cars, you can stand.' He gulped and dutifully stood with a pirouette movement and adjusted his jacket and trousers and offered his chair.

'Lack of respect for my rank and sex rankles Mr James. Shall we start again.' She placed her joined hands on the desk, wheeled closer and smiled up at him as he stood at the head of the table. He beamed back, pleased that the tension had passed, she was smiling and he had a great view of her chest.

'Here is the rental agreement and copy of the driving licence as requested' a buff folder was slid along the table. Grace offered a deferential wave to Harper who swiftly stopped smirking, shook himself back into the world of the police, opened the folder and laid out the contents in a logical order using the ferrule and rubber end of his pencil. There was silence and then the manager offered his appraisal.

'Online order, collected in person a week ago, rental expires today, cash payment with a credit card imprint as guarantee.' The manager started nervously then found his rhythm. 'Nothing unusual, we don't get so many cash payments for personal hire, more often on the commercial stuff; builders, couriers that don't have accounts. I served the lady myself and didn't think anything was odd.' He paused gaining confidence. 'What was the problem, what has she done?' His question was ignored, Grace may have considered answering but they had got off on the wrong foot and he kept looking at her chest.

Harper turned the buff folder around and pushed it towards Grace and with the tip of his pencil he pointed at an area at the bottom of each document. She took his pencil and on the inside sleeve of the folder she started to write. Slowly at first and then with a practiced hand more quickly. She straightened up tilted her head slightly to the left and studied her work and turned the folder back one hundred and eighty degrees to Harper. He then copied her actions exactly, a complete facsimile right down to the tilting of the head to study his work. He turned the folder so they could both see the result. The manager, bemused, strained to see. He could see the repeated signatures, copied from the hire agreement and licence. All the attempts were good, they got better with each attempt as the writing descended down the folder.

'I think you win this time ma'am.'

'I think we are both better than that one' said Grace jabbing towards the signature on the hire document.

'Oh no' groaned the manager 'she's not nicked it; not again!' He paused and let one leg collapse, rolled his eyes and let his arms rise and fall against his legs. 'Head office will go spare. Again!'

'Let's have a look at your CCTV son, I hope it is a good shot.'

The dejected manager headed for the door. 'Yep follow me and I will show you what we have got.'

The three of them moved into the main office area and to a desk towards the rear and the manager took the only seat behind the PC and started to type away.

'Due to the number of thefts from this branch the CCTV was updated and so we have a good shot.' He sat back and let the digital recording play. It was a good quality, nice and clear but it could only have been improved with audio. Due to the whole transaction being carried out at the main counter they had good view of Louise hiring the car. However, as the camera provided the first really clear view of Louise, stood still at the counter, Harper leaned forward and offered a nasal snort, raised his eyebrows and shook his head slightly. Grace just smiled. They watched for five minutes and finally saw the manager offer a set of keys and gesture towards a door that led the customer out to the yard where the car was no doubt waiting.

'We have this as well' said the manager bringing up another window and another camera view of the rear of their premises. That quality was not so good but Grace and Harper had seen enough. More than enough.

They both raised themselves from their stance of looking at the PC and faced each other squarely and exchanged knowing looks.

'Just come back to your office a second' requested Grace and she led the way then stood aside as the three of them entered and then she closed the door. No one sat down.

'You recognised her Harps?'

'Yes ma'am, Carole Stokes.'

'That's her', Grace nodded enthusiastically. 'I knew the face but couldn't get the name. I hope you noticed cash in a sealed envelope, and the credit card and licence wasn't in her hand bag.'

'Licence wasn't even folded' interjected Harper.

'So we think someone had just handed her the cash, credit card and licence to use here.' No one countered that suggestion but Grace did not pause to let anyone enter a rhetorical debate. She turned to the manager Grace noticed his eyes dart upwards. 'Do you have CCTV facing the road.' He looked blank, or more blank than normal. 'If you have CCTV facing the road it may have captured someone handing those documents to the person who used them to hire the car.' He got the gist.

'No, sorry just the two I showed you and a general one covering the office, nothing facing the road.'

'The credit card was not hers. Why did it work?'

'Not hers, it all tied up with the same name and signature' offered the manager?'

'They were all stolen. The person hiring the car was not Louise Byrd.'

'As a cash transaction I only took an imprint of the card, we didn't debit it. If the card was stopped then nothing would show till we went to take some cash from it.'

Harper and Grace exchanged looks and seemed eager to move on.

'I will send a PC to take your statement and a copy of the CCTV shortly' said Grace as Harper closed the buff folder and tucked it under his arm.

'Oh, and before I go', Grace stepped closer to the rather dejected looking manager who was thinking his job was on the line for losing another car 'if a policewoman turns up to take your statement, offer her a chair, offer her coffee and don't stare at her chest.' She glared for a long second then smiled and thanked him for his time and they left.

'You enjoy that ma'am' chuckled Harper as he stood waiting on the pavement.

'Yes Harper I did, I don't like bad manners, he should have offered me a seat and it was like he was a bloody baby looking for his next feed. Anyway, let's get back on this as we are getting somewhere. We can check out the CCTV in the area but I would rather get Carole to tell us.' She looked at her watch that was heading past nine. She is still going to be in bed at this time, you do know where she lives?'

'She lives near to you ma'am.'

'She does? I am not sure if I should be pleased that high class hookers live near me. Should I be flattered?'

Harper frowned. 'I wouldn't say she was high class ma'am.' Grace moved off towards the car and said over her shoulder. 'You say the sweetest things Harper.'

Thirty Two

Lou kept to the course that Carl had set. He wanted to head south and when Lou was happy that the smoother seas, chart and depth gauge indicated safer passage she headed further south. She copied his instructions and actions of sailing to a course, regularly checking the GPS and plotting their location on the chart. She would dip down into the cabin whilst the wheel was lashed and check he was still breathing, plot the position and on occasion grab some food. The fridge and cupboards had an array of hand friendly food, pasties, pastries, soups. As the evening drew in she put on the navigation lights and was pleased with her achievements but was disappointed with many things.

She wanted Carl to be awake. She had resolved to wait an hour and if he showed no improvement to call a May Day. The hour had come and gone. She resolved to wait longer, then set one day as the deadline. She realised that the moving deadline just meant that she didn't want to make that May Day. She was disappointed that she could be callous enough to wait for him to die. Better that than to give him over to the police.

She wanted him to be awake so that he could help her sail. She was making progress but she knew that he could trim the sails and get more from the boat. She had more to learn and wanted her teacher.

She was disappointed with herself. Why was she now running away with the bank's cash. She should call the police and stop all this madness. She knew right from wrong and felt the guilt, the sin of the damned. Only a few hours ago she was righteous and awaiting salvation. Now she was as guilty as he was.

The guilt and worry were shaken off and she sailed. In the here-and-now this felt good. She was in sole control, doing something that days ago she would not have dreamed she was capable of. If she could sail all night, then what next, where could she go, what could stop her. While she wanted Carl to wake, she was also becoming aware that she could cope if he didn't. She could cope with much more than she thought.

But then he stirred. He moaned and rolled and settled back into unconsciousness. She shouted down into the saloon but he slept on until it was past midnight. She was focussed on the sea at that time, it was making a soothing swooshing and fizzing sound as the prow broke the waves into myriad bubbles that swept down the flanks of the boat to gather around the stern and fluoresce, gleam and fade away and then he was coming up the stairs exploring the back of his head with his finger tips.

'Hello sleepy head.'

'More like bloody head.' He wedged himself into the corner of the cockpit and continued to feel his head.

'What happened, did I get hit by the boom or something?'

'No you fell backwards down the stairs and hit your head on the worktop. Scared the shit out of me. Blood everywhere. It looked like a baby seal had wandered into a Canadian baseball game. You will be glad to know that I cleaned the floor and worktop.'

'You have done lots more than that. I looked at the chart before coming up. I have been out for hours.'

He seemed proud. The unsaid item hung in the air. He looked at her with a pained expression and smiled. He almost looked tearful.

'You.' He paused and was looking for the words. 'You, didn't radio in.'

'No, I just kept going. I am not sure where you were heading so kept in deep water, we were in some shallows, *races* was marked on the chart and we were in those and it was really rough and that is when you fell. I have stayed deeper and headed south. The navigation lights are on and I haven't been close to other ships and have kept the chart updated with lat and long in case I needed to call for help. But I kept going.' She stopped, hoping for his validation and some praise and she got it.

'You have done really well. God you have done well and everything looks fine. He gestured at the sails. But you could have called for help.'

'I thought you would get better.'

'No I mean help for you, help to get off, to get out of this.' He still held that nearly tearful look. He just waited for the reply. All he got was a look that held his gaze, a smile and a shrug and if it had not been so dark he would have seen a tear run down her face.

'Do you actually feel OK, as I have put some paracetamol out for you and you have not eaten since breakfast?'

'Well I feel like I have a foot pump attached to my head, but I am hungry, so I think I will follow nurse Louise's instructions and have some food and pain killers. Do you want me to take the wheel though as you have been at it for hours.' But before she could answer 'actually scrub that, you can stay on the wheel, you have proved you are more than capable and to be honest if I take over I will be a liability at the moment. Let me get some food for us both and get some painkillers down instead.' He closed his eyes and held his head for a while, she could see that he was gingerly feeling his scalp to find where the break in the skull or skin was. She was happy that he would only find a break in the skin and his hands lingered at the back of his head sampling the damage. Whilst still surveying his phrenology he said, 'your course is great and I know the coastal islands around here well. If you keep on the wheel I can find one we can anchor at. We can stop, get cleaned up and you can have a sleep tomorrow. You are more than capable of sailing all night.' He said that without seeking validation. It was a statement. He slid from his seat and she soon heard the clatter of kettle on cooker. She was glad he was awake and was glad to have received his praise but the most pleasing thing was to be exploring her capabilities. She surveyed the horizon. Lighthouses flashed way off to the left, there were navigation lights way off to the right and when they were at the crest of a wave she could see a crescent moon was rising ahead. At this moment in time, in that space, she did not know which of those disparate lights could mark the limits of her capabilities.

Thirty Three

Carole Stokes did live near Grace, in a very well appointed Georgian town house that had long ago been divided into large flats. She was known to the police for prostitution but was not typical. She was not a drug user and had not been through the revolving door at the magistrates, shoplifting, soliciting, drug possession, non payment of fines and then around again. Most high class hookers just tended not to be a smack head but some treated the job as a profession and tried to keep on the right side of the law as much as they could. Living that intercostal world between criminality and the law abiding meant that Carole Stokes was useful. Harper explained on the way that, although Carole was not a registered informant of his, he knew that she had passed information to and from people if there was something in it for her. Grace had never met her before, but Harper suggested that she should take the lead, and so it was Grace who rang the bell. You didn't hear it ring but dimness came over the spy hole and let Grace know they were being inspected and she lifted her warrant card towards the glass circle in the dark wooden door.

'Carole, could we have a word?'

Bolts and locks were moved and the door opened on a chain and a hand, rather well manicured, appeared close to the door jamb.

'Can I have a look at your warrant cards please?'

'Sure' and Grace collected Harper's too and passed them on.

'Sergeant Harper, I didn't notice you' came a cheerful voice 'one moment.'

The door closed slightly, there was a jangle of

chain and then the door swung open, held wide by Carole who handed back the warrant cards.

'You just caught me I was off to the gym, apologies for the outfit.' She closed the door behind them all and they headed towards, what they understood to be, the living room and she asked 'coffee or tea?'

She looked like she was off to the gym but had no need to apologise for the way she looked. The shortest of shorts and the shortest of tops. Her dark hair was tied back and her make up, was subtly applied, she wore the cleanest trainers Grace had ever seen, but she anticipated that they had been used as she was sure that Carole did not get a body like that by being a couch potato. Grace looked her up and down as she stopped in the kitchen to boil the kettle. She looked to have known her way around a swimming pool or perhaps the ballet barre either way it was all muscle, bone or breasts.

'We thought you might be having a lie in' suggested Grace.

Carole offered a little laugh and turned from the kettle gesturing to the living room and a sofa. 'I have a sedentary occupation. It is an occupational hazard, I spend plenty of time in bed.' She made wide friendly eyes at Grace 'so I try to get up and out to the gym early each day and' she gestured up and down in front of her body 'this is the prime asset of my business so it is worth investing in. I would say that you were no stranger to the gym DCI Taylor, so I'm sure you appreciate that it's a struggle fitting it in?'

Grace noticed the nice way Carole had tried to find common ground between them and had passed her a compliment, but she wasn't being sidetracked that easily.

Grace relaxed into the sofa. Carole took a seat

to her right in a tub chair and Harper perched opposite Grace on a sturdy blanket box with cushions on. All the furnishings and finish were immaculate. Grace wondered if they had *Home and Garden* for whores.

'Miss Stokes a week ago you fraudulently hired a car from the Cheltenham branch of Auto Hire.'

There was no reply but a smile.

'Have you nothing to say?'

'I wasn't sure that it was a question or a statement.'

'Did you hire a car from Auto Hire?'

'Ahh. Now that is a question and my reply is no comment.

'You were recorded on CCTV.'

'I think you are suggesting that someone who looked like me was recorded and you mentioned 'fraudulently' hiring a car and that implies pretence. If a licence with photo ID was used then I guess, purely hypothetically, that who ever looked at the licence and the hiree, confused those two people. If you don't mind me saying, I don't think that your suggestion that I look like someone who looks like me will hold water.'

'Perhaps you would prefer to discuss hypotheticals at the police station?' Grace stood up but Harper stayed seated and so did Carole.

'Of course DCI Taylor I will come to the station but my responses will be no comment until Mr Davidson is able to attend and I'm sure at that point you can discuss your suspicions with him whilst I'm released. I will come with you but suspect it will waste your time. This job does afford me plenty of free time; it won't be *I* that is inconvenienced.'

Dodgy Davidson was a good criminal lawyer.

He got his clients out of the custody suite quickly and often planted the arresting officers with a plethora of complaints and writs for their trouble. Grace would call him herself if she were in trouble, if she could afford it. Grace was about to get frustrated, most criminals would offer something rather than get pulled into custody, it just looked like Carole would miss her appointment with the personal trainer. No big loss.

Harper made a dejected sigh and spoke in a consolatory style, 'Carole, we don't want to take you in as we are in a rush. I am sure you will help us when you know what's at stake. We have your prints on the hire agreement.' *A blatant lie, but a beautiful one* thought Grace, 'and know who asked you to hire it. We just need your confirmation.'

Carole seemed not to have heard the question and turned from Grace to Harper, 'Sergeant Harper, it has been a while, I hope the wife is well?'

'She is fine, Carole; we do need your help.'

'I don't want to comment on this.'

'Are you scared of what might happen if you tell us?'

'No, not at all. If you have my prints then I may have to face some music but this is more about honesty amongst thieves, if you pardon the expression.' She gave Harper an apologetic smile. 'I have helped you before and you have helped *me* before and I do remember your wife being very nice to me as well, but this is just something that I don't need to tell you more about.'

Harper turned from Carole after smiling back at her and then looked across at Grace. 'Ma'am, I would suggest we just tell Carole what we know, lay it all out and trust her to make her mind up whether to help or not.'

Grace stood and walked behind the sofa. The room was much larger than her own living room, large Georgian windows, framed by lovely heavy curtains that were swagged back to let in the maximum light. The bookshelf was cultured and orderly and the books actually looked like they had been read. Everything was in its place apart from a rather nice cocktail dress that was draped over a windsor chair and a pair of fabulous looking shoes akimbo beneath it. They looked to have been kicked there and the dress dropped onto the seat after an early morning arrival. Grace came to a decision and gave in.

'Can I help you make the coffees?'

Thirty Four

A few hours after dawn they neared some low duney islands off the French Coast. Carl engaged the engine, dropped the sails and they motored slowly into a bay. It was deserted, not because of the hour but because of the location and from the driftwood and flotsam on the beach it looked like no one had ever stepped ashore here before. But Carl had been here before and took Louise through the theory of anchoring and let her take the wheel and bring them in. She waved when the echo sounder showed ten meters and the chain and anchor ran out. She moved the boat astern and they felt the anchor hold. A kedge was let go from the rear and both anchors held them in place in the bay. The engine was stopped and they had splendid isolation.

'You OK?' he asked.

'I shouldn't be as I have been up all day and night but I feel OK. How is the head?'

'OK as well actually. I think it will be better without this crap on it' and to prove his point he pulled some dried blood out of his hair.

'My plan is to have a swim, this beach is great for swimming and the Gulf Stream makes it like a Jacuzzi and then a fresh water shower. If it is OK with you I will get you to actually wash out the wound with warm water in the shower and then we can get a dressing on it.' He was rummaging in a locker in the cockpit and pulled out a folding ladder that neatly fitted over the transom. 'And then we breakfast, sleep and head around the headland to a nice little port to take on water. How is that for a plan for a day?' He was already out of his harness, boots and jacket. Louise watched as his tee shirt came off.

'Seriously, we are going for a swim?'

'It's a good way to get clean after sailing in the same clothes for days and it's good to get some exercise. Finally, it would be good in case I pass out as you can pull me ashore. I take it you can swim?'

'I swim very well, I just didn't expect to be going for a swim.'

'Well this trip is all about the unexpected.' He dropped his trousers but thankfully kept his boxers on. And with that he put one hand on the roof of the boat and hopped high in the air so that both feet cleared the guardrail and he clutched his knees to his chest and disappeared. As the splash subsided all was silent and Lou stood in wonder waiting.

It was splashing on the far side of the boat that caught her attention and she saw him striking out powerfully towards the headland, keeping parallel to the shore.

She did enjoy swimming and had swum to a good standard at university and she *was* at the beach. As Carl was heading away she felt confident enough to strip down to panties and bra and then went towards the ladder, then decided against that and made a good dive from the deck into the water. After a while she did feel warm and it was good to get the muscles working. She swam in the opposite direction for a short while then did not like the fact that she could not see Carl. She swam back to the boat and under it as Carl had done and then followed his course for a long while, returned and trod water for a while and then headed into the beach.

She lay in the shallows on her back, propped up on her elbows. There was no swell but the smallest of waves lifted and dropped her as they passed under her.

She ran her hands through her hair and enjoyed the little heat that there was in the early morning sunshine.

Carl continued to swim. He has a good stroke. Something different in it that suited sea swimming. She was confident that over a short course she would be quicker. He was working his feet too hard. Too much splash. She swam like a swan, as long as it was a swan in a pool. He was headed towards her.

He felt his feet hit the sand and stood up and caught his breath and started up the beach. She was reclined and looking rather lovely. Her panties and bra were more revealing than she probably wanted them to be, they clearly were not made for bathing. He was sure that she was feeling the cold too. And perhaps he was as well. He stayed with the water above his waist and adjusted his boxers.

'You look like a mermaid.'

'You look like crap, you have blood running down your face from your hair.'

'Good', he raised his hand and had a feel about 'it feels much better. You swim well.'

'I swam for the university. I don't get much chance to keep it up now.'

'Perhaps that will change' he came towards her in a stooped movement through the shallows that concealed his erection and he splashed down next to her, face down. 'This is the beach I told you about. I can leave you here. You can hide the cash and tomorrow if you cross the island you can reach civilisation and I can get away.'

She stayed reclined, letting the water run around her. She looked into his face. He looked very serious. She had not been thinking about leaving until then.

Perhaps she should get back to normality now that he was not going to die on her. But then he continued.

'Or stay with me. Come with me. Sail with me and we can swim off the boat on beaches like this time and time again. If it had not been for you yesterday I expect I would have drifted into the coast and died, or be in custody. You saved me from that. I can see that' he thought for a while, 'I need you and I think I would miss you if you were not here.'

'Carl, this is all a bit surreal. Swimming off a yacht on a beach in France when I should be cleaning my flat, thinking about work or shopping in Tesco. I shouldn't be here sailing and; enjoying myself.'

'Why don't you just stay for now and you can just say when you want to go. I won't argue. Whatever happens we both know that this started out with you being here under duress and I will have to be extra nice to make that up to you.' He smiled and she couldn't help but smile back and she nodded gently. 'Race you back. It can be university against combined forces.' He raised himself up by pushing her shoulder and thus held her down and got a good head start.

'Not fair you cheat!' She went into butterfly through the shallows and then some of her best front crawl and started to slap his feet within meters of the boat.

'OK you win, after you' he offered her the ladder 'and you get first dibs in the shower. He looked at something he really shouldn't have as she climbed up the ladder in front of him.

'I do think there is a bikini on board, I will dig it out. Let me get the shower running but don't hang about as there is not too much fresh water.'

Carl stowed things out of the way in the shower

so that it was less of a toilet and more of a shower, although a small one, put out soap and shampoo and got out of the way to let Louise in and then he closed the door.

There was no lock, which on a small boat would have been pointless, you would know when someone was using the toilet so she decided to listen to the instruction to "not hang about" and opted for speed. She set the water running and took off all her clothes and stepped into the still cold shower when the door opened.

Carl, towel in hand, stopped sharply when he saw her naked. His mouth moved wordlessly and she turned away from him. 'Sorry. You were quicker than I expected. I have a towel.' He did look shocked but did not move, he just seemed to take in the form of her body. 'Look; I will close my eyes, can you just clean out this wound and I will get out of your way.'

He placed the towel onto a high shelf and then closed his eyes and stepped in closing the door behind him. She shied further away from him and he, with eyes closed got under the shower, turned to get water into the back of his head and then fumbled for the shampoo. Their bodies bumped as he moved under the shower and they stood and moved back to back. He was focussed on washing and she hesitantly continued to rinse.

'Ow, ow, ow.' He winced as he had clearly rubbed the wrong part of his head. 'That's the tender bit. My eyes are still tight closed but will you have a look at it?'

He backed away and bent at the waist so that she could inspect his head. She had to fully turn to face him and she moved under the shower and gently moved his sodden hair from the area that he was indicating held the cut.

'Well this is not uncomfortable at all. You should have said you were going to join me.' She played the water onto the wound and put some shampoo into her palm.

'I didn't think you would be naked, you were too quick for me. Sorry, I didn't think. If it helps I will be naked too.' He didn't give her a chance to argue and pulled down his boxers and reached for the soap. She laughed as he hopped from one foot to the other and noticed the difficulty that he had getting his pants off over his cock.

'I thought you had your eyes closed.'

'Tightly.'

'There are two cuts, close together and both closed up, it is not gaping and they look clean. You will live.'

'Will you kiss it better?'

'Don't push your luck sailor boy.'

He was still bent over letting her wash his hair and he was judiciously cleaning his legs. He put the soap down and put his hands onto her hips before raising himself upright. He still had his eyes closed. Not that that made much difference when he stopped at chest level and began to kiss her breasts.

He then stood upright, pulled her towards him and kissed her mouth. He drew back slightly and whispered 'have you got your eyes closed now?'

Thirty Five

The faux formality of coffee making took the tension out of the moment and Harper stood back and let Grace and Carole get on with making his coffee. He knew Carole from when she had started in this business with a pimp and black eyes. The pimp had been knifed and she had gone freelance but there was no connecting those seeming fortuitous events although she had come into some money along the way. Fortune favours the brave perhaps.

Grace offered up some small talk and Carole freely entered into conversation on ground coffee and percolators. They exchanged a few glances and smiles and Harper could see them relax. He liked the tactic. As Grace pushed slowly down on the cafetiere's plunger watching the grains, water and coffee mingle, spiral away and separate. She took a deep breath and made a decision to trust Carole and not to treat her as the suspect she was.

'I should have known from the locks on the door that you wouldn't take risks, you don't know me from Adam and why would you want to help, where's the upside for you? If I can explain where I am you can then decide if you want to help.' Grace finally looked up from the cafetiere and smiled at Carole.

'We know it was Carl Richardson who asked you to hire the car.' Not a flicker of surprise crossed Carole's eyes. 'We have the CCTV from the business that covers the corner of the road where he gave you the licence and cash. We know that he paid you to pose as Louise Byrd and to hire the car in her name. What did he say that made you do it?'

Carole offered a tight lipped smile and turned

her head downwards and to the right slightly but said nothing. She was still not in a place where she wanted to offer information. Her body language said 'no comment.' Without missing a beat Grace read that and continued.

'Carl Richardson carried out an armed robbery yesterday, threats were made and shots were fired. He took Louise Byrd as a hostage, the person you hired the car for.' Something caused Carole to move at that point, she had held her cool and not shown surprise but that last fact had meant something to her. 'He has implicated you in robbery and kidnap; or perhaps worse. I don't suspect that you knew what he was going to do with the car, or do with the girl. You don't want to get mixed up in whatever he is doing to Louise; kidnap, rape, murder?' Grace let the accusations hang and saw Carole pondering something. She did not want to fill the silence and so turned with cup in hand and headed from the kitchen back to the sofa. She sat and waited, Harper arrived and gave her a subtle wink, she took it to be affirmation on her actions.

Carole followed and sat in her previous chair and spoke.

'I'm not an informer and I would rather say nothing but I think I do need to help Carl and myself, out here as you have this all wrong. I met Carl at the Dawn Club. He was a nice guy. In my profession you get to discern the nice from the' she paused and took a breath, from a less stoic person you would think she was gathering courage, 'less nice. He helped me out with someone who was giving me problems. I used to go there as it was open late and on some nights I didn't want to be alone. He understood that. He would respect that. He would chat and we had an affinity. He was aloof but close. One night he saw that I was being bothered but by someone who I could not be bothered by and he dealt with it well. The police would call it cuffed, he sorted it out without causing problems. He came to be someone who could sort things out without you really noticing. He was unobtrusive and I loved that in him.' She looked up at that, she had seemed to be studying the swirling spiral within her coffee, she looked between them, she seemed to have noted, as they had, that she had referred to Carl in the past tense.

'He knew what I did'

She faltered and focussed on the spiral again.

'...my profession and he helped me when I asked. Clients who did not pay, or those who...'

She faltered again. Grace and Harper waited, bated, to hear about the man they sought, to find out what he was, who he was.

'...treated me badly. But he was not the type to break legs. That is not what I wanted, he could fix things, be persuasive and I liked him for that and we trusted each other. That is a rarity. We became friends.' She stopped, looking at each of them in turn, getting their eye contact for a split second to emphasise what she said next 'no sex, just friends. But to the nub of it; he has clearly gone now and he lied to me over why he wanted the car hired. He didn't want me involved in this, he wanted to protect me. He told me his girlfriend needed to be collected from the airport and he was going to hire a car, but he had nine points on his licence and they wouldn't hire him one. He just asked me to pretend to be her so that he could get a car in her name. He would, drive it to the airport and collect her. I thought it strange but he had her licence and said that he did not want her to have to try to hire a car in the early hours of the morning at the airport. He didn't want it in my own name as they were off to her parent's for a week. No hint of armed robbery or kidnap. It's just his girlfriend.'

Grace and Harper looked at each other and weighed up the implications.

'Louise Byrd is his girlfriend?'

'That is what he told me, so' she leaned back into her chair and took a sip of coffee 'I believed him and I thought I was actually doing them a favour. As far as I could see he couldn't hire a car due to his convictions and she couldn't as she had left her licence behind. Nothing untoward, nothing bad, none of this kidnap and I don't think he has murder on his mind.'

Grace and Harper couldn't help but look at one another with open mouths and Harper spoke. Slowly. And not to anyone in particular.

'So he knew her. Knew her well. It is an inside job. She has not been kidnapped. She isn't in danger. They are in this together. They are on the run.'

He came forward and put his elbows on his knees and cradled his coffee in both hands and smiled down at the granules left at the bottom of his mug. He shook his head slowly from one side to the other.

'I knew her pants were there for a reason.' He looked up slowly at Carole to explain.

'We found some of Louise's stuff at Carl's house, her pants for example, that indicated that they knew each other. Do you know where they both might be now Carole?'

Carole looked across without moving and her eyes rolled up as she thought.

'No, I don't.'

'Bit of an unfair question though Carole' added Harper standing up 'if you did know, you wouldn't tell us.'

He smiled down at her in a respectful way and she laughed and smiled back.

'As much as I like you Mr Harper, if I did know where he was, I wouldn't tell you. Some people, I see naked and I *really* see them, what they are really like. I can tell the good from the bad and know some I would give up to you. I would happily tell you what I know. With him. If I knew where he was, I would not tell you. If they are both free and happy, then let them be.'

Thirty Six

They motored from the bay. She steered the course prescribed and he busied himself on deck tidying in only that way that a skipper about to come into port can. Skippers knew that there would be expectant eyes, critical eyes, looking at and into your boat. Looking at the warps, sheets, fenders and ties with either criticism or ambivalence. He beat the furled mainsail into place and he returned to her and looked at the depth gauge, his watch, swept the horizon and then ducked below. He seated himself at the chart table. She couldn't see what he was doing other than more continued tidying and the sorting of documents. He returned to her again.

'Are you nervous; is this going to be OK?'

He nodded at the wheel instead of answering and she stood back as he took the helm.

'The port we are heading for is just an outpost, but they get sailing tourists as it is great for sailors and their own small crabbing fleet. Very Briton and I don't think they are looking for fugitives from a robbery in England. I have been here several times before. It will be fine.'

They had headed out to sea, past the headland and were heading into a dark mark set against the low dunes. A low lighthouse indicated the harbour entrance and it stood at the end of a short breakwater that embraced a few fishing boats tied to algae covered buoys. He slowed further as they passed the breakwater entrance and he quickly surveyed the scene for a berth then swung toward a floating pontoon-come walkway and glided into place.

Louise stepped ashore when bidden and passed

a rope around a bollard. She stood back as Carl busied himself with mooring fore and aft and retied the rope that Louise had first used. She looked along the pontoon to where a bridge went up to the breakwater itself and then the breakwater headed towards a few close knit houses. She could see a café and shops and a few people milling about. Mainly people going about their business of fishing or passing the time of day. One man, who emerged from a heavily windowed wooden shack set into breakwater seemed content that his business involved them and was slowly heading their way. Carl raised a genial hand while the man was still on the breakwater.

'Harbourmaster; I will go and have a chat. Can you kill the engine?' He strode off and she stepped onto the boat and busied herself with the ignition. When she stood up she watched as Carl opened his arms wide in welcome and launched into rapid French. The words were lost due to the distance and the language but from their body language, free laughter, the pointing at the dressing on his head and back slapping she felt that these were two people who know each other through casual acquaintance and were pleased to have met again. Their discussion, initially loud had quietened down and may have entered into a formal discussion, how long they were staying perhaps, where they were going, where to buy food whilst Carl delved into a pocket. As he did so he looked back towards her and raised a hand. She raised a hand and the harbourmaster looked in her direction whilst chatting but he did not wave, his hand was held out toward Carl. He pulled something from his pocket and then moved so that his back was fully towards her. She could not see what was being transacted but both men were looking down at whatever had been passed between them. In a moment it was over and the harbourmaster had handed it back and Carl's hand was within his pocket again. Both men backed away, still chatting and waving whilst they headed in opposite directions. Louise was puzzled as she had thought that she had glimpsed what had been handed across to the harbourmaster. It was just a flash but the colour was unmistakable. Had Carl really handed over two passports for inspection?

<u>Thirty Seven</u>

Ice cream seemed the only thing to sate the puzzles and so Grace and Harper had presented their "goodbyes" and "thanks" and headed, in some quiet (apart from one outgoing call made by Grace) to the park and were now slowly scraping layers of strawberry and chocolate ice cream.

It was Grace's place to speak first, rank has it's privileges, and Harper hung back. 'That was a convincing presentation, I do believe what Carole said, especially' and an empty spoon was pointed at this point 'that she initially didn't want to comment on anything but I have a niggling thought somewhere on this. She could be convinced that she was told a lie. She could be truthfully recounting what Carl had said to her, but it could still all be lies.'

'But, why go to those lengths ma'am, why not just pay her to rent the car and say nothing. No lies no patois. Feeding her that tale wouldn't achieve anything; unless he knew we would trace the car and the renter. All a bit tenuous, isn't it just more likely that this is the truth. We do have evidence', Harper raised both tub and spoon and opened his hands as much as he could in submission, whilst slowly shaking his head, eyes closed, 'and I know that that evidence may be circumstantial, but it is still there and shouldn't be ignored, of her possessions at his house with her fingerprints. Carole just elaborated on our, well mine at least, view that they are in this together.'

'Well we have had no ransom demand and no body. If we do say unequivocally that it is an inside job and she does turn up in a ditch we are going to look stupid.' Grace wagged a spoon before reassembling the carton's components and putting it in the bin 'but if that happens we won't know if it was a kidnap gone wrong or just thieves falling out and then we would actually feel stupid. Hang on, here it comes.' Grace pulled a vibrating phone from her pocket and Harper could see that she was reading a text. He could also see that it was a perplexing text. She pursed her lips and moved them over her teeth, just as if they were ideas being moved about her brain, shuffling theories, pushing motives and reasoning to make room for others. He continued to watch as her nose wrinkled, she still looked at the phone but she was not focussed on it, that was now elsewhere and her eyes now widened and moved as more thought crowded in. He could tell that these thoughts were routed from the call she had made to the station on the drive to the park for the ice cream. He sat patiently, having the patience of a saint and the prescience of a devil held him in good stead in his career.

'He does have nine points on his licence and he wouldn't have been able to hire a car with those. That part of the story holds true. So he wanted to hire a car, not steal one, the reason for that is obvious, he needed to leave it on the road and in the open for some time and he did that to ensure a good escape route. He must have put the car in just the place he wanted some time before he needed it and wanted to ensure that it looked in order. But that meant that he needed someone to hire it for him. Really anyone would have done.' She sat back and Harper felt a question was coming his way by the quizzical look on her face, but it would be a rhetorical one. 'Of all the people he could have approached to ask them to hire a car he chose Carole. Of all the people! He had mates from the services, who told me they would do anything for him, even his mild mannered neighbour would have done it, so why approach Carole?'

Harper didn't hesitate 'she seems to be the only female he has in his life. He wanted the car to be hired by a woman and he had no one else to ask.'

Grace leaned forward and nodded slowly in full approval at the implied reasoning and his tacit agreement with her own theory. 'If he and Louise were planning this together then she would have hired the car herself. He went to some lengths to concoct a plausible story that Carole seems to believe.' She put her phone into the inside breast pocket of her jacket and swivelled towards Harper and looked at him for the first time in a while and focus came back into the here and now, 'but the one thing that is odd is to hire the car in Louise's name, to get her name into the frame and imply that this is an inside job, they had to have her driving licence. How did that happen?'

Thirty Eight

Carl sauntered back, the sea legs, moving pontoon and his happiness to be in France combined with the way things were playing out had put a joy into his step.

'Let's just lock her up and go and get something to eat, there is a little café in the harbour and let's just pass a few hours away over lunch' he smiled and closed his eyes as he said the words. She beamed back at him filled with the wonder of it all and caught in the contagion of his enthusiasm. He stepped down into the cockpit and busied himself with the door and hatch, 'we will have to do some shopping and get fresh water before preparing for this evening's tide but we have hours to burn before that.'

He visually checked the warps as they passed and headed along the pontoon towards the hamlet at the end of the breakwater, he turned towards her and took her hand as they started to walk and his gentle squeeze was returned. The breakwater was manufactured from large rocks, smoothed with age and bound together with gritty mortar, their irregular shapes led to pitfalls and rises and they walked like children avoiding the pavement cracks. They moved apart and together as they rocked and stepped along as if pushed by turbulent waves and laughed if they crashed together. She clutched his left hand in her right and grasped his bicep with her left and hung on till they finally reached shore and the path smoothed. With practiced steps he led her to a café with a scattering of tables outside and they sat facing the sea. A waitress arrived promptly and he started to babble away. Louise picked up the odd word. The fluency and vocabulary was beyond her schooling and the waitress's words were completely lost to her masked behind an additional layer of accented nuance. She simply revelled in his enjoyment of being able to do something else that he enjoyed, his teeth shone in his smile as the conversation moved. Lou couldn't work out if he enjoyed the speaking or understanding more but noted some familiarity between them and with a flourish and some quick questions and answers the order and conversation was wrapped and he smartly turned all his attention back to Louise.

'I have eaten here before and have ordered a range of things so I am sure that between us we will have plenty to eat, it isn't an extensive menu, mainly fish, would you believe' he widened his eyes in mock surprise. 'But it is all fabulous so they are just going to bring out a few courses.' He sat back with some self satisfaction he was looking pleased with himself. And why not. He looked around, he was sat with a beautiful woman whom he had just made love to for the first time. He could see his own yacht moored ahead of him and he could compare the lines and curves of the boat and woman. He could try to find fault in either and find none. He was in his second favourite country, was sat in the sun and a rich dark coffee and a cool beer had just been put in front of him. He voiced his thanks in a language he had learned to love and launched himself upright with a flick of his back, sat in the edge of his chair, and took up his beer and offered it to Louise and said 'a votre santé.' He smiled down at her as their bottles made the slightest of touches she said 'cheers' in reply and then he rested back into his chair and drank.

'I am just going round the corner for a paper' he stood, turned and talked at the same time and said as he retreated from her. 'I won't be five minutes' and he raised his hand and moved out of sight.

The sun was climbing with the heat and the tide

was receding, he could see a leisurely few hours being spent at the café through the French lunch time and then they could shop for fresh food, put on water and prepare to depart. He was interested in the papers though and would be interested in what English language papers they took and how old they were. He doubted he would find what he was looking for in any French paper.

He walked into the cool of an empty paper shop and asked the rather hairy lady behind the till whether they had any English papers. He received direction and she waded from behind the counter to inspect the papers with him. He took up a day old Telegraph with some pleasure and delved into his pockets for a roll of Euros and suggested she keep the small change. He said his goodbye while looking at the paper and exiting the shop. He was pleased that they were not front page news. Page three was the next facing page and held the second tier stories, still nothing, nor page two. He continued to flick through the pages whilst he walked back to join Louise. He walked slowly as he was in no rush and was reading whilst walking. He slowly glided into his seat checked the date of the paper again, took a swig of coffee and turned another page.

The first course of calamari arrived and he put the paper away and told Louise of the bearded lady who served him. He joked that he had no musto remover on board and it could be a long voyage. Did she have plans to grow a beard? She stated that she would if he stopped shaving and then they agreed that neither would sport beards. They ate and drank their way through the starter and he told her of his plan.

'The Atlantic is a big sail, potentially nothing for miles but we will head south towards the Canaries for two reasons; one they are lovely islands and if the weather is not great we can stop there and resupply and two if we are being tracked then we can pass through the Canaries and carry on without stopping and confuse any followers. But so far' he stretched over the remains of their food for the paper 'I can't see that we have made the papers so don't expect a massed squadron of boats after us.' He took up the paper while eating remnant chips from his second course.

'But here we are! We have made the press, way down on page eight. My mum would be proud.' He sat reading for a while while Louise jockeyed for position to also see the story, but he began reading in hushed tones.

"Cheltenham armed robbery an inside job. Sources close to senior officers confirmed yesterday that the police are searching for a man and a woman in connection with the armed robbery of Lloyds bank in Cheltenham. A female member of staff is alleged to have let an armed man enter the bank and steal thousands in cash. The police have asked for Carl Richardson, thirty eight, an ex-soldier and pub doorman to contact the police to eliminate himself from enquiries. Both the unnamed cashier and Mr Richardson have not been seen since making their escape from the rear of the bank by motorcycle. Police are concerned for the twenty two year old cashier's safety and are appealing for witnesses". Carl let the paper fall against the table and leaned in towards Louise and lowered his voice even more.

'They think you are involved in this. They think that you, you planned this with me. The inside man.' He offered a concerned look. 'I am sorry, I seem to have got you into more trouble than I expected. Why would they think you are involved in this? Don't they see that I just took you as a hostage?' He looked back at the paper as if it might hold some answers and then passed the paper to

Louise. 'They are looking for you as much as they are looking for me…wow.' He gave a shrug, but on the bright side perhaps that means that they are not pursuing us both as much as they might.' He turned back towards her and she looked up from the paper as he leaned in again conspiratorially 'yeah, I thought that they would really pull out all the stops to find a kidnapped, young girl; but if they think you are also a bank robber then it takes on a different perspective, they are just looking for two thieves and not a victim of a kidnap. Perhaps it has taken the heat off and relegated this to page eight. Wow.' He sat back in his chair and finished his coffee.

He thought for a while. Perhaps they had got clean away? He always feared that had the balloon gone up, with radar and the Navy on their arse they would be captured, but the police had seen it as just a robbery and then their resources would be different. Perhaps they had been forgotten about already. Page eight today, twelve tomorrow then just a memory. He smiled ruefully, finished his beer and suggested they order more beer with their dessert. She replied with a surprise question.

'Don't you need a passport to come into France?' It was as rhetorical as it was provocative. For a split second she saw shock flowing over his face, from his mouth opening, his head sharply moving backwards and then his eyes widening, but he masked them with moving effortlessly into a gently chuckle.

'Of course, *you* should have one, but I know the harbourmaster well. He and I go back a while and I always show him mine. I told him that we had come this way on a whim and a good wind, in preference to the Channel Isles. I suggested that you stayed on board if it was a problem and he saw it as the joke that it was rather than a serious suggestion.' He had regained full composure again and swivelled towards her 'and this is an outpost where they make their own rules. Claude and I have shared a cognac or two before and they don't see me as too much of an outsider. It might be different in other countries, I am sure that in the Caribbean, where they are used to cruising sailors we will be fine without passports. I expect that I can get one sorted out for you at some point if we have to. You can choose your country. Perhaps if I teach you enough French we can make you French?'

They smiled at one another as the final pastry course arrived and then as they were both nearly replete they slowly made inroads into their puddings and then relaxed into the chairs and stretched out their bodies to accept the warmth of the sun. Eventually Carl looked at the bill and produced a roll of Euros and tucked notes under the empty beer glass and put his head through the door and spoke to the waitress and waved goodbye. They walked slowly back to the boat hand in hand and slept in each other's arms on the saloon benches for an hour.

Before dropping off, Carl thought again about how the plan was coming together so well. He counted off his good fortune and then he had a surprising thought. It hit him for the first time and he was surprised that he had not thought about it before. It was the type of thought that many people have on many days but it took him unawares, it wasn't something he had thought about for a while. He had simply wondered how much money he had. Perhaps, as he had his own bank cashier, he should find out how much cash he had stolen.

Thirty Nine

Guy Chambers was a good probationary constable. He had racked up a few complaints for being heavy handed. That showed he was getting involved and did not shy away from the more dangerous or violent situations. The number of his arrests showed that he was good at sorting things out without dragging bodies into the cells unnecessarily. Being able to defuse situations and deal with problems with diplomacy, which could involve using his rather imposing bulk and deep West Country voice, was much more preferable than the paper-work and time wasting of locking up, cautioning and releasing gobby speeding motorists. Guy was waiting for Grace and Harper on their return and was chatting easily to another officer. He was still in full uniform despite his shift ending an hour ago. Harper waved him into Grace's office and they all arranged themselves into the room. Harper sat in the back corner and Guy moved the chair he took towards the wall, so that he could easily see both Grace and Harper. Harper led the conversation.

'Thanks for staying on PC Chambers. You know that we are leading the enquiry into the Lloyds bank robbery, we think that you met both the people involved.' Guy looked suitably surprised, he edged back in his chair his back even more straight. He nodded slowly in mock agreement.

'Are they known to us as I can't say that I know anyone suspected of armed robbery. You do know I have only been here eight months?'

'We think it might have been just a fortuitous meeting, they are both completely clean, as far as we can tell. You may not remember them but we hope you do.'

Guy nodded again to show his agreement and also hoped he remembered. This could be turning into a job interview. He knew he was going to be asked a direct question shortly and if he messed up he had a great chance to look a complete twat. He didn't have to wait too long for the question.

'On 28th September last year you went to the Dawn Club in response to a report of a theft of a handbag. The victim,' Guy and Grace noticed the strange inflection on the word victim, 'was a Louise Byrd but we believe it isn't going to be on your top-ten most memorable jobs as the bag was found in the club by a doorman there. Can you tell us everything you remember of that shout?'

Guy felt like he was at the end of a hospital pass. He was back on the school playing field seeing the muddy ball looping down towards him, along with a large pack of muscle, sinew and anger following very close behind. As he had done in his school days, and was going to do now, he handled the situation by focussing only on the ball, catching it and heading towards the goal line.

'Yes, I remember it, have you got the name of the doorman, I know most of them by name now.' He pulled his moleskin out of his breast pocket with practiced ease and moved to the date Harper stated.

'01.03 am, PC Garner and I attended though she was outside, Louise Jane Byrd, Flat 8 17 Lansdown Road. She was a bit drunk but was perfectly lucid, I was talking to her when' he referred to his notes 'Carl Richardson, 59 Jersey Street came along with the bag. He told me that he had found it in the ladies toilet. She had a look through it to see what had gone missing. She didn't have much cash to go missing. She said it was not worth the insurance claim. I talked to Mr Richardson about interior CCTV and he said there was plenty on the bar, doors but none specifically on the toilet areas and none on the area that Miss Byrd had been sitting. He said we could have the tapes but it seemed like a needle in a haystack plus on a Saturday night, at that club, we would have plenty of known suspects on the guest list. But she was understanding and not worried about what she had lost.' He stopped. He looked between Grace and Harper and waited for the next direct question. He knew it would be coming. Grace provided it.

'Do you think Louise Byrd knew Carl Richardson?'

He pondered a while and then said without equivocation.

'No, they didn't.'

'Anything else,' Harper delved with a double barrelled question, 'anything unusual?'

'It was a very routine job on a quiet Saturday night. All over in' he looked at his notes again 'eight minutes. It only sticks in the memory as she was good looking and it was one of my early Saturday nights on the job so I was all eyes and ears. One thing that occurred to me just now though is that I have not seen him again. I think he was forces but I have not seen him working doors since. That's a little strange.'

Grace was quietly impressed, other probationer's attempt at recall of minor events from months ago would not have been so fruitful, but she hoped he would have the information that they really wanted from him, 'do you know what was actually stolen?'

He referred to his notes again, they could see his eyes scanning the page, flicking down the lines and then he reeled off a short list.

'I remember the bag was cleared out, nigh on empty and the reported loss' he looked at his notebook, 'was approximately twenty pounds in cash and change, passport and driving licence.' He heard the silence and noticed Grace and Harper exchange quick looks and he suddenly felt self conscious and recognised that he had said something of import. He also misjudged the situation and thought he had made a mistake and their exchanged glance was to ensure the other had spotted it. He tried to recover.

'I did tell her that she would have to report the loss to the DVLA and the Passport Agency.'

Forty

The day moved leisurely into evening. They had walked back into the village and stocked up on fresh food. That had all been stowed and then Carl had talked Louise through how to charge the water and diesel tanks. Then they had shared another shower in the marina's facilities as Carl had said it was going to be the last time they would have an opportunity for a while. Perhaps their next shower would be on another continent. And then they waited for the tide. They sat in the cockpit eating apples and drinking black coffee. He had brought the cushions up from the saloon to air and it made a comfy nest for them both to rest upon and she leaned gently upon him and their angle left them gazing at the stars and listening to the low noises from the boats about and village life.

They chatted easily about sailing. She had many questions and he had plenty of answers. They chatted about her family. He had many questions and she had plenty of answers. It was something that he seemed to have missed out on and he wanted to absorb family from her. He listened to tales of Christmases and cousins and then apologised.

'I have taken you away from them and I am sorry. I love you being here, but after reading the paper I know that the police think you're involved, I'm sure your parents wouldn't believe that. We can send them a letter from an island in the Caribbean to let them know what actually happened and letting them know you're OK.' He moved around in their nest so that he was no longer beneath her and took up a position so that he could look at her 'and you know you can leave if you want to. I would like you to stay, this crossing is going to be a real test and I expect that I will need you, but you don't have to come.'

She held his arm, the one that was around her shoulder, thick and muscular, she repeatedly stroked the short hair so that it lay smooth and flat on his arm.

'No, I don't want to go. I want to stay and I want to sail.' She looked up to the stars as she said that. 'I had a mundane nine to five in a bank. Nothing of interest from one week to the next, then wham! I meet you and I think it is fair to say that it has been interesting since then.'

'Sorry about that.' He kissed her temple.

'Well, I am slowly forgiving you.' He kissed her again and felt the moisture of his last kiss had remained in place.

He rested back upon the cushion nest and turned his body beneath her so that he could look her in the eye a little easier and passed on an easy smile.

'Many years ago I saw a programme on TV, I think it was an Open University programme. There were these guys with beards and sandals, it was all in black and white, and it was about psychology. What I learned from that stuck with me. What they were doing was an experiment on a baby chimp. It was a tiny pathetic little thing. More fluff and wide eyes than anything else. It was in a small cage and all alone. They experimented by putting various things into the cage. They wanted to see how it would react. It was so small, alone and frightened that most of the things they put in the cage it would cower away from, mirrors, toys, rubber balls. But that little monkey would explore its world when they gave it a metal frame covered in fur. All it needed was something to hold onto. That metal and fluff form was enough for it to hug and hold, it had enough substance to allow the little monkey to feel safe and to have something to return to if it was scared. That little monkey had a comfy monkey to reassure it. When the researchers took away the comfy monkey the little chimp would become timid again. With the comfy monkey in the cage it would explore and be happy. Most of us need something, family, husband, wife, job to give them security so that they are free to explore. I remembered that experiment after I left the army. I didn't feel scared, just alone, more alone than ever before. I didn't expect you to be here with me Louise, but now that you are I feel so much safer.' He gave her a squeeze. The contradictory message of a large, muscular man, who could have squeezed the life out of her slight frame, feeling safer because she was there, bemused her but she remained silent as she could see, hear and feel the sincerity in his words.

'You're my comfy monkey Lou.' He kissed her temple again. 'I always hoped that they returned that tiny monkey to its mother at the end of that test so that it could feel some reciprocal love, not just the warmth of some fur.' He was silent for a short while and then urged her to stand.

'Well enough lounging about. Time and tide!' They both stood and started to busy themselves to get the tide that would lead them across the Atlantic. He sang melodiously with happiness and headed off towards the foredeck. Louise stopped for a while. It was a sad tale about the monkey, caged, alone and the subject of experiments. Was it ever returned to its loved ones, or just disposed of when it was no longer of interest. It left her uneasy. But she resolved then and there to put it out of her mind. She smiled broadly at the thought of the adventure ahead and got down to the task.

She wanted to step on the cockpit seat and head forward but first picked up Carl's jacket that was on the seat. She took hold of the collar with her right hand and lifted it high and swept her left hand toward it and folded it over the crook of her arm. She stepped out of the cockpit and went towards the main mast.

'You might be needing this.'

As he reached out for it she felt some movement within the jacket and something dropped onto the deck. They both looked down but he dropped onto his haunches quickly and swept up the two passports that had fallen from his inside jacket pocket.

'It's handy having two' he stuffed them both into his trouser pocket 'some country's visa departments can hang onto them a long time.' He paused and smiled a nervous smile. 'Glad they didn't go over the side. I better stow them below.' He headed off towards the rear of the boat then turned.

'You carry on with removing the ties and we will get the mainsail up.'

Lou murmured her agreement. Any two passports would look the same. Burgundy cover, gilt coat of arms embossed on the front. Familiar and comforting font and capitalised PASSPORT. Those two were very different, one was crisp, clean and fresh and the other was worn, the gilt lion and unicorn almost obliterated as if it had been used regularly, handled and shown as ID most weekends, as if it had been carried in a handbag for years, tumbled with the other contents and become rubbed and bashed. In fact that worn out passport was just like her very own one.

Forty One

Grace and Harper stood beside the hire car Carl had dumped. It should have been a great day to be out of the office. They stood in strong sunshine looking at a cold trail. Unbeknownst to them, they had stopped at the same toilets as Carl and Lou had done during their trip only days before. Harper had stood there looking at the same scene; the vale and sheep, the oaks and walls and he thought about his retirement and walking through country such as this. He day-dreamed of stopping at B&B's, hostels and the occasional four star hotel (with spa) to receive some luxury treatment and remind himself that years of hard work and the occasional beating meant he did deserve a retirement of treats and leisure. But no need to go too mad, he liked the variation, frugality and fun of B&B's.

He was trying to focus now, the heat was not so intense beside the river and they caught some shadow from the trees. The local CID approached and provided a welcome with a heavy welsh accent.

'I am DC Dai Jones. You made good time.' The voice was Richard Burton's the figure was more Elizabeth Taylor's. Clearly plenty of Welsh lamb had been imbibed over a considerable time in the force. He wore a suit and shirt too tightly. Harper recognised the look. An old school copper in his last few months on the job. Perhaps the farewell drinks and meals had started and there was no point in buying more work suits and shirts at this point. Grace saw the signs too. As the old DC's gaze spent too long sizing her up and lingering where she thought it shouldn't. Her day and the case was going badly enough and she hoped their liaison officer was still up to the job.

'Was reported as suspicious yesterday at 16.07 by a sailor who moors on this pontoon', DC Jones pointed using a biro through the trees and down to a sleek, blue, yacht. 'He arrived here after a week away and the car was parked in his own space. He didn't recognise it and saw it was a hire car and called them and the hire company called us. We then rang you and here we are.' He waved an expansive hand at the scene, like an estate agent who had just opened a door onto a dismal room. 'We got our boys to pop the locks.' He dipped his head and leaned in, clearly to impart some knowledge of interest 'they popped the central locking with an electronic gizmo, wasn't long ago' he brazenly looked at Harper at this point 'that we would have put the window in with a truncheon, but there you are, times change. We kept our hands off as much as possible, but there is no body in the boot. You can have a good look yourself but no getting in without getting white suited. Only thing I can see is the passenger side door release has been removed. I believe you were working on this as a hostage taking?'

'Hmm, that's right' offered Grace as she stepped forward and bent down to look at the door handle.

Jones stepped back and noted Grace's skirt ride up as she bent down. 'Well you don't have to be Sherlock Holmes, or should I say in these modern times, have a degree in criminology and be on the fast track', Jones tried to share a conspiratorial wink with Harper at that pointed remark, Grace just rolled her eyes, 'to see why the guy cut the door handle off. She was placed in the passenger seat with no obvious way out. We reckon a snip with bolt cutters was used to cut the handle off and the child lock is on the rear doors.'

Grace and Harper circled the car looking into

the open doors and boot. They took their time. Jones circled too in silence, primarily to take in more of Grace's charms when the chance arose. They rendezvoused at the boot.

'Not much to go on for you I am afraid. There are lots of footprints here about, too many to help you' shrugged the Welshman pushing on sunglasses. 'You want us to get it into the lab and give the pointy heads some fun?' Grace and Harper exchanged looks.

'What did you make of it ma'am.'

'As it is a hire car it should have come to them clean as a whistle, it was in his possession for two days before the job. We knew the mileage from the booking form and deducting that from the current mileage and comparing it with our own getting here I would say he did hardly any miles at home and then drove here. I think it is reasonable that he drove home, put stuff in the boot, placed the car where he wanted it; and after all, that is the reason he rented it, so that he could leave it exactly where he needed it, and then they drove here. There are long hairs on the passenger's side and one on the driver's side. They are slightly different colours. The one on the driver's side will be Carole's as she must have driven it from the hire company. There are some muddy footprints in both foot wells. Not mud from this track, but not far away. In an almost spotless boot there are what look like crumbs. I reckon they did what we did on the way here ourselves Harper, stopped for a sandwich and a piss. The marks in the floor of the boot carpet are indistinct but *as I do* have a first in criminology' Grace turned towards Jones at this point 'and *am on the fast track* to becoming Sherlock Holmes with tits, then I would say he had several boxes in there, some of which were heavy plus what could have been a cool box. With the positioning here next to the jetty, I would say' she looked through the trees down to the water's edge with some dejection 'that they have both pissed off abroad.'

Jones spoke first with a quizzical note. 'But we are getting guys arranged to sweep the woods. I thought we would be looking for the girl's body around here, or perhaps somewhere on route between Cheltenham and here. The door handle shows she was taken against her will. What makes you think she has gone abroad with him?'

Grace walked a few paces towards the steps leading down to the jetty and then turned before continuing down. 'A few things. I suspect these are her foot prints. The day she was taken we know it rained here but it has been dry since and I don't think there are too many sailors using the jetty wearing heels. They come and go as well, so she was not dragged down and thrown in. She has walked up and down, helping with the loading of provisions perhaps. But the most obvious thing', she headed down the steps 'she has her passport.'

Forty Two

They sailed long into the first night. The shallows were left behind, then the small coastal ships, then stars and navigation lights came on and the moon rose into the embrace of a warm evening sky that retained an ethereal light as the moon and water bounced the light between them. The few coastal lights ebbed out quickly and the two of them traded lights as one or the other spotted or tracked vessels. They would work out what ships carried that type of light and their headings and kept a weather eye on them but these too petered out. Lighthouses were the last easily recognisable thing. Along the French coast they marked their passage and as each dimmed and flashed no more Carl and Lou recognised the fare wind was taking them further from this shore and closer to another. They took turns to sail and with a soft wind and smooth sea the time off the wheel was easily spent. Lou made hot chocolate and toast in the early hours but their day on land had meant that they had little tidying to do.

'Time for you to turn in?' suggested Carl.

'I seem to have a second wind after that cocoa and this is still so magical' she looked at the merging of sun and sky at the horizon, delineated only by a magical star spangled dome to show where the water wasn't.

'It is pretty good tonight. Dawn will be something special too.' She checked her watch. She hadn't looked at it for some time. 'It's stopped.' She gave it a tap and looked at the misty dial and frozen hands. Carl felt he should say something as she sounded a little saddened.

'Oh dear.' He paused she was still looking at it

and rubbing the glass. 'Did it have sentimental value?'

'Not sure you can get attached to a three quid watch from Esso. If it was a loving gift you'd still think that the cheapskate could have at least splashed out in Argos. It only reminded me of why I have it. It just used to remind me of how late I was for the next thing I had to rush to, or how long I had to wait to get out of work. It is just another type of manacle on your wrist.' She undid it and without looking or moving anything but her right wrist it was flicked over her shoulder. There wasn't even a splash to mark its passing.

'Tempus fugit.' He saw her, or perhaps felt her smiling in the darkness. He reached out a hand and they held hands for a few seconds till he needed it back on the wheel.

'There is another watch in the chart table drawer. It might be a bit butch for you but it is waterproof. If you need it then help yourself.'

'Did you get it from a garage for 99p?'

'No, from a dive shop for a few hundred.'

'I will wait till we get more diesel.'

'Talking of work, what you could do to pass the time and become all useful for once, you can count my money.'

'Your money!' Lou's fake surprise was good and loud.

'Correction darling, *our* money. Have a look and see if you can afford to get a decent watch at our next landfall. I have no idea how much *we*', Carl exaggerated, 'have. We might be able to stretch to something better than a garage watch. The holdall is under the starboard bunk.'

Lou got up jauntily belying the hour. 'I am only

counting the money for old time's sake. To remind me that clock watching and working for a living are a thing of the past.'

She put on the kettle, took off her jacket, readied a pen and paper and hauled the holdall out from under the bunk and set it down near to the saloon table. She unzipped the large topmost zip, adjusted the lamp and removed the largest denominations first. She had an expert eye and arranged the sealed bundles in blocks and was able to count the blocks and note the sum total on the pad. With each denomination total shown it was easy to get a grand total at a glance. Some would have stopped there but the bag also contained loose notes and without thinking she bundled and counted those when others may have just stopped. The remaining loose change accounted for just short of three hundred pounds. The bundled, banded and sealed blocks totalled just short of a hundred thousand.

She replaced the cash back into the bag and on the table remained several disquieting things. As she had emptied the bag she came across the tools of Carl's trade on the day that he had earned the cash. It was memories that she would rather not have unpacked. The table held the slip of paper with her totals, a coil of piano wire, pliers and one thing she had taken out of the bag early in the count. It was the gun that had been held at her head. She was surprised at the weight of the thing. She had lifted it out and placed it far away from herself, not sure of how safe things such as that were. She got up and made tea and resolved to put the memories away. The pliers and wire went into the tool box below the saloon steps. She wanted to put the gun over the side but instead considered that she needn't worry and left it where it was and headed topside to see the dawn.

'Tea and biscuits. That will cost you ninety eight thousand, three hundred and fifty pounds.'

'That much'! Carl beamed. 'We can live like kings on that. I know of a few places in the Pacific where money like that would buy an island and everything on it. Wow. Well we will have to be a bit careful not to blow it all on watches, shoes and girl stuff, but we can do a lot with that amount.' He gave her a one armed hug as they both stood at the wheel and looked towards the bow. 'You OK princess?' He gave her a squeeze and looked down at her with concern.

'Yep, it is just that as I went through it I found your gun and it brought some of it back.'

He moved quickly away from the wheel and put both arms around her and held her close. She reached out a spare hand and steadied the wheel. His head was buried in her hair and she felt him breathing deeply and liked the feeling of her hair moving in the warmth of his breath. He pulled back and looked at her.

'Sorry, I forgot that was even in there. I just didn't think, the thoughts that made me do all of that are so anathema to me now I didn't even remember that I had a gun down there.'

'I didn't know what to do with it. I was going to throw it over.' He laughed and pulled back further so that now he looked at her from arm's length and smiled.

'I am glad you didn't as we couldn't pick up another one of those from the garage.' He took a swig of tea, put a whole biscuit into his mouth and headed below.

He was only a few seconds; he had clearly just picked up the gun and returned to the cockpit, still chewing biscuit. Once again he was holding a gun, but as he ruminated and tried to keep crumbs and biscuit within his mouth he did not look menacing.

'We could put it over the side, but it's a good gun. It is loaded but is safe.' He held it by the barrel, though at an angle so that the muzzle was away from them both and offered it to Lou. The gesture he used was almost demanding and she took it with little hesitation but once she held it she felt the trepidation.

'I will take the wheel, you keep the business end of that pointed to windward, we don't want a hole in the hull, or in me.' He checked and guided Lou as she seemed to be a little pre-occupied and holding her wrist he guided her hand to point towards the dawn light.

'In European waters all-is-well but as we get into the Caribbean and Pacific we might be glad to have a gun aboard. Piracy is one thing but common theft is more likely and we might want that to even up the numbers. There is no point in having it for the protection of the boat if we don't both know how to use it. Point the gun down into the sea and pull the trigger.'

Lou didn't move. He had taught her how most things aboard the boat worked to some degree or another. This seemed, in some way to be like another lesson. It was not too dissimilar to them getting the flares out and him telling her about their usage. And he was probably right about it being good to have a gun on board if they were going to far flung lands where they could hardly go to the police themselves if *they* were robbed. She pulled the trigger. Nothing happened. She tried again.

'Safety is on. I wouldn't have given it to you if it wasn't. It is important to feel what that is like. If you ever take the safety off then you had better be looking down the barrel at someone you want to kill. And make sure I am behind you. I don't want to make you proficient in small arms. I would rather just put it away. But I want you to just know that you can fire it safely if you ever need to.' She looked at him briefly and he launched into instructions and she turned and looked down the barrel. She thought he was running through a checklist that he had provided to recruits many times before, on stance, arms, focus, releasing safety catches and breathing. His voice changed and he regressed into a different person that barked orders in a staccato. His voice slowly rose and resulted in a call to fire. She pulled the trigger and despite the steady stance and taut frame the gun punched back and leapt upwards with a red flash and resounding bang. The smell lingered for a second as her ears rang and then they left the gun smoke and noise behind them as they sailed on.

'Getting the safety on is the reverse of the release, always ensure it is on before you do anything else.' He leaned towards her and took the gun from her and looked it over. 'Two things to remember. You know nothing about guns and it is best to keep it that way. No more lessons. At some point I will clean and oil it but we will put it in the locker over the chart table. Let's hope that we never get to see it again.' He descended heavily and turned back towards her as he slid the gun far into a locker that was high above the chart table.

'The second thing is that you're going to have more chance of hitting someone on this boat by throwing the gun at them than firing at them. I think you even managed to miss the sea.'

<u>Forty Three</u>

'I think we have lost them Harps. This is the end of the trail. Physically and metaphorically.'

Harper had followed Grace down the steep bank and onto the jetty. He walked slowly. He'd known as soon as they had taken the call advising where the getaway car had been found that they'd lost. With no body in the boot and a car at an empty quay it just left them with another option to search the sea as well as the land. That was hopeless.

She seemed relaxed and happy as he approached, perhaps the pressure to find a solution was over now. It was all over. She kicked off her shoes and sat down and dangled her feet over the water. Harper saw the years fall from her. Compared to him she was not old to start with. Sometimes, when she was going at full chat, on the top of her game in a big enquiry (that was itself in full tilt) she took on authority and respect that added years to her. On days like that he could see the Chief Constable in her. Not so much her father, though that was there, but the fact that she herself would one day be that role. Of course he had seen a few come and go. He had seen a few rise in the ranks in the early days but now they were appointed from outside their force with regularity and by the time they knew a few names of the coppers, let alone the villains they were off to Majorca to retire. She might be different. She was good at what she did and he hoped to keep working with her. Despite cases such as this that looked to have no results. None that were good. She kicked her feet and leaned a little forward and pointed her toes so that she just touched the surface. On days like this though, she looked like a little girl to be cared for.

'Don't go falling in.' He sat beside her and was glad that she sat back from the treacherous angle she had been at and that she pulled her skirt back to a decent length.

'I will talk to the coastguard and see if they have any way to trace shipping from here. Perhaps we will get lucky.'

'I doubt it, not had much so far.'

'I suspect it is a long shot as I don't know if they can tell one blip from another or if they keep records but I will give it a try.'

It was quiet for a while and then she turned to him and smiled. 'Where do you think he will dump her?' Harper looked shocked so she continued. 'You don't think he will just dump her overboard at some point? It would be easier than a shallow grave. No trace if weighted and deep enough. I just don't think he needs her anymore.'

'You ever sailed ma'am?' Grace shook her head at the water and then turned to listen. 'I went to the Channel Isles with my brother-in-law. Pissed with rain, freezing cold, no sleep and he was a complete arse. The only redeeming feature was he was not my brother-in-law at the time as he brought his sister who I had never met. She became Mrs Harper. She was great company and made the trip something that I will treasure for the rest of my life. So will he have brought her all this way to just save digging a shallow grave; I don't think so. From what we know she is bright, attractive and liked. Let's hope that he, despite being a criminal that we would like to kick the shit out of, is half decent.' Grace looked away down towards the sea and he kept looking at her and liked the way the wind moved her hair. 'And there is a lot to be said about two people being cooped up together for a length of time. A bond forms.' Grace continued to look out to sea and without turning she said 'are you still talking about Mrs Harper?'

'Yes ma'am.'

'Good.' She paused for a minute and then continued. 'This isn't the end Harper' she held her head low and swivelled it towards him, one eye was closed against the reflection of the sun from the water. 'From the off this guy has been leaving false trails to implicate Louise but after looking at the car and that door handle we can know for certain that she was brought here against her will. If she were involved he wouldn't need to take a hatchet to the door handles. That was a big mistake as now we know that this is not only robbery but a kidnap. The chief is not going to be happy that the trail has gone cold but we now know that this is an abduction. If you thought that we would be cuffing this and boxing everything up, think again. We know they were here' and with that she swung around and lifted both arms that had been straight and firmly supporting her as she sat on the jetty and pointed with both hands out towards the mouth of the estuary and to the open sea, 'and we know they went that away. We need to talk to the Coastguard and be detectives, and work out where he has taken her.'

Forty Four

As they headed southward the heat climbed with the barometer. The winds became softer as if they were tired themselves from the warmth of the day. The days lengthened and took on a regularity that the weather and unfamiliarity had not allowed previously. Despite the provision of auto pilot they stayed close to the wheel. Perhaps it was their comfy monkey. It was certainly more comfortable when they pulled out the bench cushions from below and lounged in the cockpit. Clothes had lost their necessity to protect against wind, rain and cold. They wore loose shirts to protect from the worst of the sun at noon and often dispensed with every stitch for lengths of the day. That led to an afternoon ritual of sex and snoozes. This avoided the heat of the day, allowed them to catch up with sleep and provided a very engaging diversionary task in the afternoons.

Mornings were more ordered with cleaning and any maintenance. One still morning, when the sails hung unmoving in the warm air, Carl had readied some tools and placed the small ladder over the transom and happily busied himself renaming the boat. Lou leaned upon the pulpit rails and looked down at him working and they easily chatted and she occasionally passed something to him. He carefully removed and moved letters from *Appeal* and then Carl announced, 'I name this ship Apple. God bless her and all who sail in her!'

Lou gave an impromptu trumpet salute, popped into the galley for a cool beer and splashed a few foamy drops from the bottle over the letters before toasting the boat and passing the bottle to Carl.

'Not a bad job'. He was pleased with his

planning on this. The vinyl letters had peeled off and been reapplied once the hull had been prepared and he had added an image of an apple to mask the slight fading where the redundant letter had been.

That had been a lazy day but ordinarily they both worked out. This was limited to pushups and sit ups on deck and pull ups from the boom but Carl threw in enough Yoga and Pilates plus liberal encouragement to see a real improvement in Lou's physique. All the ups had pulled things in, though they joked that her beer belly was proving stubborn. Navigation was a regular event to plot progress. With the distance they were travelling a detailed chart wasn't required but they recorded their latest position on a chart with a small scale. Each day their mark moved a small way across the blue paper and pacified their thoughts of ever seeing land again. Their electronic plotter counted down the days till landfall. That ETA was important as they had bypassed the Azores. That Mid-Atlantic stop off point would have been too obvious a place to check should anyone have considered that they were crossing the Atlantic. As a get-away went Carl was happy that his was almost complete, but starving to death on the crossing would not crown his achievement. He was used to rationing and had overstocked and continued to use the store cupboard carefully to ensure they made things last. He also knew that each of them could afford to lose a few pounds. She more than he.

But he had fallen for her. He knew that he would if given the chance. She was beautiful, young, vivacious and bright. He continued to teach his ready and able student more on navigation and sailing whenever the opportunity arose. They both became adept at caring for their vessel. He revelled in her inquisitive nature and the time spent discussing and talking about sailing, life and travelling made their time together pass easily. They spent some time apart too. Into the afternoon, after lunch they would often read apart or sail alone. Each recognised a bit of down time was required. Then one would seek the other out and one would take the other in their arms and after awhile make love. The evenings started with a meal. They took it in turns to create something different from the dry ingredients with varying success. The meal would be late in the day and be taken on the rear deck. Afterwards they would drink tea and cover themselves with blankets as the sun dipped. The warmth of their tan and sunburn would reverberate from the wool. And then they would talk and look up. Periodically a star would shoot and they wonder that they were the only ones to have seen that moment of glory. Their privilege of time and place to see a spectacle of wonder before it was gone forever. Southern constellations started to appear and reveal sights that they had never seen. Then one would sleep (dependant on the weather and any shipping) and the other would sail, or on calm, clear nights they would both wrap themselves together till dawn.

Then one morning, clear beautiful and bright, Louise arose and then promptly threw up over the side.

Forty Five

The coastguard was not as Grace expected. The Gloucestershire force had no recurring needs to pop to the coast, it came to them in the shape of the Severn Bore pushing some seaweed and seals up the Bristol Channel. Hardly cause to think of lifeboats, salt spray, rugged coast line. So she had a mental picture of bearded men in woolly jumpers, big binoculars, sat in a room with many windows facing a vast sea. She and Harper were ushered into a windowless room off the coastguard station's new reception. Lots of reflective glass and pot plants and the only sea to be seen was in the background of a poster about the disposal of flares; and that was a drawing. But the coastguard himself was in nautical uniform, dark trousers with a white shirt that held epaulettes and embroidered insignia. He did not sport a beard, he had a wedding band instead she reasoned. He exuded an air of quiet authority that led her to imagine him having been on the bridge of a ship for many years before washing up here. He was warm in his welcome and took them to a coffee machine where she thanked him for seeing them at short notice and he made small talk about finding the place and him trying to help out as much as he could. They had talked on the phone so he had the gist of what they wanted. They returned to the small room and he made a short detour that resulted in his appearing in the room with a chart and a sheaf of A4 papers. He spread out the chart to reveal a colourful pattern, symbols, shapes, numbers, letters and lines. Little made sense at first glance and Harper and Grace tried to work out what was land and what was sea.

'This is where you were earlier' he pointed with a

tip of a pencil 'all this is good anchorage but without amenities or harbourmasters or anything of that nature. That stretch of coast has many rias that provide great anchorages and easy access to the open sea. Very popular with sailors. There is a voluntary scheme for registering voyage details but we have nothing from that location for his boat, which is called Appeal.' He passed a sheet of A4 across to Grace who took it with some surprise.

'This is his?' She looked at a picture that seemed to have come from an aquatic estate agent.

'Yes, bought and registered in his name in October last year. VHF radios need a licence and he has one. Boats have a MMSI number, just like a car number plate and can be electronically tracked, but it is not mandated for a yacht of that size. But he did register it. He might be wanted by the police, but he seems to be OK with the coastguard. With the boat's name known we were able to contact the previous owner and got that from the broker who sold it on. Contact details there.' He leaned over the table and pointed with his pencil to the contact details on the flyer. 'I let the broker know that you might be in contact. I know of them, but don't know them, too far away. Good reputation and from our discussion it was a nice well equipped and sound boat. The broker told me', he broke off and looked cautiously between them, his eyes flicking from Grace to Harper and back to Grace, 'and I hope you didn't mind my asking, I just thought it would help you out trying to track them, what the buyer wanted from the boat.' Grace raised both palms to him and shaking her head voiced her complete agreement.

'No you're the man for that job, I am sure the two of you could have a more sensible conversation on that topic, you're the experts.'

'Well we did spend some time talking tackle and fitting out. The broker's view was that your man knew what he wanted and made a good decision on the boat and timing. Right at the end of the season, paying good money for a well fitted out boat and then he went on to upgrade the electronics, service the engine and renew the sails before he collected it. The broker and I agreed that that kind of preparation and the tale that he passed onto the broker of what he was looking for in a boat all points to him doing serious sailing. Additionally, he collected the boat alone. He had told the broker of the boats he was interested in and why. He wanted something he could sail short handed.' He looked between them again and explained 'that means on his own or with little crew and that he could take into deep water. The broker does not remember him mentioning any destinations or even where he planned to moor her. I did not tell him why you were interested in the guy. But the broker did tell me that he had met the buyer twice, when he came to view the boat and again when he came to collect it. They had talked extensively about the requirements, choosing this boat, negotiations and then the after-sale kitting out. Sounded like he was a good customer and paid promptly. No doubt you will want to chat to him yourselves.'

They all looked at one another as the coastguard paused. They had an expectation as he built up his part and led them to the reason that they had all met here today.

'So', he paused again and rubbed his hands together and then rose to his feet so that he could lean over the chart and see it from their perspective 'where might the little tinker have gone to. We do know this. He left here some time after 17:00. From what I know of the guy', he looked up from the chart towards them, 'which is not much' he looked down again and pencil pointed 'he sounds clearly competent so would have left with the tide and on the day in question it turned just before 17:00. You made the same drive today so it would have been doable, but wouldn't have allowed for too much hanging about. I can certainly put him at this spot.' They all focussed on his pencil point. 'He was definitely here.' The pencil pointed to the gap between two headlands, the headlands that they had both seen earlier that day when they looked from the jetty towards the English Channel. 'From here I am guessing. We do have records of the radar and MMSI tracks of all the vessels in the area. As this is a small vessel, travelling on the bank holiday weekend, on the turn of the tide, from a busy anchorage area; well we can not tell from the tracks who is who. Most of the yacht shipping that we can trace headed south. Some went towards Ireland, some westwards. Let's discount them. If this is a getaway then heading for Cardiff wouldn't be bright. The wind was not good for Ireland. Unless you think that the guy wanted to go there I would say it was unlikely. If he wanted some distance and was not too worried where that would lead then going south has more options. You see there was a good wind coming for those heading south. Nice, steady and strong and would allow him to get some miles under the keel. Also, the best track to take keeps you well clear of Lands End, a bit like getting on the M25, there is plenty of traffic all heading the same way, but the traffic could be going anywhere.' He moved the pencil swiftly across the map. 'You could swing past Lands End and up channel, lots of busy ports all along our coast and many more on the

French coast. If he kept going south you can swing to the Channel Isles. Good sailing if you are competent, but this guy wouldn't want a UK port and I would suggest that heading up the Channel would be counter intuitive. I think that in that boat, fitted out like that, he would be in the boats that we tracked past Lands End heading for West France. Our radar horizon runs out by then but in the time I have had I have talked to colleagues and we have plenty of shipping heading that way. It's the way to go if you want to go anywhere warm. We lose track of any prospect of trailing them due to their size and their mixing with other shipping. What I can tell you is that with the prevailing wind and size of boat, barring any mishaps, they would be around here in a day.' He put a faint circle on the map South of Lands End. He paused and then drew a much larger circle off the coast of France 'and in two days he could be anywhere in here, if he did, in fact, head south at all.'

'That's a big circle' said Harper looking up from the chart at the coastguard who then straightened up and looked down at them with some dejection. 'Well the wind strengthened behind them, the tides were good, they could get some speed up in that weather and once clear of shipping rounding Ushant then' he motioned with pushing his hands away from himself and spreading his arms 'they could go off in many directions.'

Grace waited a while and asked a question. 'Where would you have gone?'

He seemed to like the question as he smiled and moved on his feet and looked at the chart with a chuckle. He thought some more then said 'nice little boat, but capable and with new sails. New sails means he didn't want to take chances on sail damage. It wouldn't matter if you're coastal sailing, you rip a sail then you just change the rig and head to port and order another, just slowly. If you're mid Atlantic then it is more of a problem as you don't want to take the risk that you have to head across slowly.'

'Mid Atlantic' said Harper? 'That's over here', and he gestured off the edge of the chart and to a blank spot on the table.

'Well you asked where I would have gone and I think that with that boat and with me knowing what I am doing in a yacht, if I had robbed a bank I would cross the Atlantic. Some might go to the Med but you are bottled up then and I think that subliminally, you would want the open ocean.'

'Why would you go South then, America is over here.' Harper pointed off the map again.

'Yep, that is the way, but with the prevailing wind and weather it is better to swing Deep South to cross. But that is bad news for you.' He frowned and sat down to break whatever the bad news was. 'You see, I wouldn't go straight across, but hug the French coast, even perhaps the Spanish, Portuguese. You could then island hop and go to the Canaries, Madeira the Azores or straight across. His deciding factor is how much food and water he has on board and how brave he is. Some like to stop off on the way.'

'Well I would say this guy is brave. An ex-marine and an armed robber so let's say he is not risk averse.' Grace leaned forward, she wanted the coastguard's best guess. 'Where is he now?'

'OK, if he is going for it; an Atlantic crossing then let's assume that he will also avoid all ports where he might be spotted so he would bypass the Azores and, if I were him head into the Caribbean islands. If he has enough food and water for the two of them for over a month then that is the place to be. Drop the white ensign and raise the stars and stripes or some other flag and merge in with the other yachts cruising the islands. I can check the wind and currents but without knowing his course we are really guessing but I would say they are well into the Atlantic now.'

'Can we track them; find them?' Harper said that in a less than hopeful way.

'They are well over the radar horizon for land based stations. You can talk to the Air Force and Navy.' Coastguard sounded excited at that prospect, but then some realism sunk in 'but it would be a bit of a needle in a haystack. And if they made contact they would need to actually get to the vessel to see if it is the boat you wanted.' He shrugged his shoulders in final resignation.

The words 'needle in a haystack' hung in the air for a while and were then followed by the less than encouraging caveat from the coastguard 'but of course, this is all guess work. They could really be anywhere.'

Forty Six

She had not been sea-sick on the whole crossing but did feel rough again that morning. Being on deck or below made no difference and she and Carl had primarily eaten the same things so he was waiting to go down with it as well. Clearly the last of the fresh food was not that fresh. She had been on the wheel for the latter part of the morning as being in the air on deck helped and she was feeling better. Well enough to try to eat something. She set the auto pilot, ducked beneath the boom to scan the empty horizon and went below. All was quiet under the fair breeze and she put the kettle on and dug out the porridge. Whilst the kettle did its work she checked the plotter and noted their current position.

As they had no definitive landfall, other than the Caribbean, they had decided to use the winds as best they could and see where that led them. As landfall was now within a few days sail the prospective marinas were presenting themselves. And it was a marina they wanted, not a secluded beach, they need to stock up, clean up and most of all get off the boat into a shower and into a proper bed.

Louise had pulled out the correct chart two days ago and although they were still off the right hand edge of it she could see where their current course would make them appear on the chart. She then just ran her hand along their course till her finger ran aground. She looked north and south and picked out a likely island that was not off their current course and seemed to have some facilities. She memorised the name and sat at the chart table. The chart table itself hinged up, like an old school desk. Beneath it were sailing paraphernalia to assist navigation and a myriad of pens, pencils, rulers and reference books. One she had looked at before was in the corner of this cubby. It was an almanac of the anchorages in the Caribbean and she wanted to ensure that this marina had the facilities they required, i.e. a yacht club with showers.

As she pulled the book from its place in the high, far, left corner, the base of the desk moved. A small section rose and fell as the heavy almanac was pulled over its edge. Boats have many such covers in the hull, cupboards and lockers. They give access to sea cocks, wiring and fastenings for deck gear but Louise had not seen or been shown this one. She rested the desk lid on her head so that she had both hands free and pushed on the board. It see-sawed and with her right hand she removed the paper-back-book sized board. Beneath it were Carl's two passports. She scooped them out, her nails dragged lazily on the board as she got her hands beneath them and she pondered that this was a good stash place and if there were more that she had yet to find.

She opened the first. It was bigger than the other in that it had more pages and she looked at his photo. A stern, unhappy look was upon his face as if the photo and application was all in preparation for a trip he did not want to take. It was some time ago and he had really close cropped hair. She fanned the pages and looked at the visas. They were for interesting and exotic places or in indecipherable languages. She liked the full page Nigerian visa. It was stamped 'Multiple' and had an extravagant flourish of a signature in a green ink.

The other, that had reminded her of her own passport, looked older due to its wear and she fanned the pages and found a US entry stamp. She smiled to see that he had been in the states at the same time she had been.

She thought it unlikely that he had spent the time in theme parks and beaches. She moved to the thick final page to check out his photo.

What she saw took her back to the photo booth that she had sat in in the Post Office. The world of noise was just outside the curtain and she had wound that seat down as if she was screwing herself to this spot and not actually setting herself free. And then she had sat, read and re-read the instructions and inserted the money. She then stared into the plate glass and critically read her face and waited for the flashes. After the third she had broken into a broad smile and released the tension and actually allowed the booth to take a photo of her real self. The other sad looking, lifeless ones were the ones that first went to school to be countersigned and then went into the post to Peterborough and then one was laminated into the passport that she lost months ago. She leaned back into the bench, the passport held open in front of her. It had been stolen months ago and now, as she sailed into the West Indies, she had found it under the chart table in Carl's boat. Her mouth was open as she tried to get some perspective but nothing came. She heard a foot fall behind her and she turned to see Carl jauntily coming through the cabin.

'You feeling bet….' He started as he saw Louise turn and look over her shoulder towards him with her mouth still open and the passport held between her thumb and first finger.

'You have my passport?'

He looked deeply at her and his mouth dropped open. Then he slowly closed it and straightened up. He seemed to grow as he put his head and shoulders back and briefly looked towards the ceiling as if for divine intervention, or inspiration. He received neither and deflated, slowly sinking downwards as his shoulders fell and rounded. He turned and sat on the saloon steps and faced towards her but with his head bowed. His elbows were on his knees and he steepled his fingers and took a position as if he was in prayer. Neither spoke as she simply waited for his explanation to come. He didn't look at her as he started his confession.

'I'll start at the beginning. I had decided that I wanted to sail the world and put all I had into this boat. I needed some additional finance and decided to just take the money I needed. I looked at several banks; I opened a few accounts and then chose your bank. I saw you when I was opening the account. You just walked past, you were late and that gave me an idea of how to get behind the counter. I watched the bank more closely and it was clear that walking; *forcing* might be a better word, forcing my way in with you would be the path of least resistance.' He looked up at her 'and I recognised you from the Dawn Club. I worked on the doors there.'

She frowned and then started, pointed her passport towards him as recollection sprung into her mind. 'God yes, I thought I knew you, did you help when my bag was stolen?' She hesitated and changed her pointing hand into a wagging gesture, 'you stole my bag. That's how you got my passport.'

'It isn't as straightforward as that.' He looked down at his hands again. 'I knew you from the bank and from the club, you were there most Thursdays and so I became interested in you. If I could use you to get into the bank then you would be useful, but all I was interested in was your timekeeping. If you stayed late in the club then you were often late for work on Friday. I just kept tabs on you, of what time you left and the time you got to work. Then one night something happened that changed my plan completely.' He looked at her without moving his head much, his eyes swivelled up to see her. 'It just kind of happened and it wasn't my intention.' She just looked perplexed.

'Go on; what "just happened"?'

'I was watching you in the club when a girl close to where you were sat started to act suspiciously. She caught my attention and I watched as she took your handbag.' He sat back and put his elbows on the stair tread behind himself so that he could be more demonstrative and he used that space to show his surprise. 'She picked it up quite brazenly and headed for the toilet. I was really angry, it actually surprised me how I felt as I was actually planning to put a gun to your head, but I felt angry that someone took your bag. It was all a bit screwed up, but I tagged on behind her until we were in the corridor heading for the ladies. Just at the fire exit door I told her to stop. I told her that I had seen what she had done. She actually tried to deny it, but I put pay to that. I took your bag off her and told her to leave and never come back. I think I was so angry that I put the fear of God into her, I shoved her out via the fire door and I was stood there with your bag. I was going to bring it straight back to you. But I didn't want to actually meet you, or to *talk* to you. So I dithered and then thought I could look into it and find your address. You see I wanted to know that as part of the planning. It would tidy things up so I crossed the corridor into the staff room and was just about to open your bag when I heard on the radio that the police had been called and I quickly said I would check the ladies. I was in a rush and just took most of the stuff out plus some cash. I really planned to get it back to you. I was just going to find your address and then I could leave it all back at your place. But what I actually did was to give you your bag back and the rest I took home and kept.' He resumed his prayer position with his hands together, she could see his contrition as he continued. 'I will admit that I felt excited to sit down and go through what I had taken. I only had seconds to take things and I didn't know what I had. But...' He seemed to struggle with something, '...you had so much in there, your bank ID, letters, driving licence, passport and things that I took to be mementos of places or people. I even had a pair of pants.'

'A girl needs spare panties sometimes' she added helpfully.

'Well, your life was in there and there was a part-written letter to a boyfriend and it said that you hated your job and wanted to travel with him again and something clicked' he put a finger to his temple to show how his idea had grown, his eyes widened and he looked imploringly at her. 'I had an idea, a crazy, demented idea, but one that grew, the idea that I could; that you would, want to travel with me. To sail with me and it has come true. You became part of the plan.'

Louise looked quizzically at him. He was still animated with his grand idea, was he really suggesting that he had freed her in some way?

'You kidnapped me. You stole me? Stole me from the bank as you thought I would like that?'

'Yes, and you do. You do, don't you?'

She exhaled sharply at the mere suggestion but couldn't respond in the negative.

'Well. I didn't. You had a gun to my head, you forced me here.'

'No! I gave you plenty of chances to go.'

'When?'

'In England, when we stopped in the rain, I kept saying you could go, but you wanted this. You wanted to stay, you wanted some excitement.'

'Excitement! That's a trip to Disneyland. Excitement is not having a gun put to your head.'

He actually looked surprised.

'Don't you want to be here, don't you want to be with me?'

'Now I am here, yes. But; why couldn't you have just asked?'

'You wouldn't have come. And I wanted you to come. I decided that I wanted someone and I chose you. It was wrong. But I realised that I could reach out and take that money' he gestured to the locker where it was stowed 'and I thought that I could reach out and take you. I planned it and I am sure that I have confused the police enough to have got away with it. What I have struggled with since I first saw you is how I can hope to enthuse you enough to want to stay with me.' He had raised his voice with the final words and looked imploringly at her. He now moved from the steps and knelt on the floor and looked up at her and gently took the passport from her, opened it and looked at her picture.

'This gave me hope. Your ticket to travel freely without let or hindrance. I saw it as a sign and I knew that many harbourmasters would want to check passports. They don't actually do anything with them. Claude in France just wants to see that you have one, I can't see that he's a great one for on-line submission of data. So I kept your passport and it has brought you here. Stay with me?'

She looked down at him. She had no choice.

She was backed into a corner.

'Of course I will.' She leaned forward into his embrace, but she couldn't bring herself to close her eyes and she looked over his shoulder at the floor.

Forty Seven

Grace sat curled up on the sofa in her flat. The standard lamp beside her was the only light and Radio Four burbled in the background. It was just some noise for company and Melvyn Bragg was trying to broaden her mind with some minutiae. Her mind was elsewhere as she was intending to work. A yellow legal pad was beside her and a checklist of items scored through and a few pages of diagrams proved that her mind had been active. She now sat contemplatively wrapped in a blanket. She had spent the day with Harper and another officer running through the case. They had started early, kept it structured, took regular breaks and assessed everything they knew on the case. Data and evidence was being filed, boxed, saved and shelved as the manpower ebbed and the investigation phase drew to its conclusion.

They had finished at a reasonable hour today, primarily as Grace and Harper were spent after the focus of the day. At its conclusion their fellow police officer had said her goodbyes and Grace powered off her laptop, closed the lid and told Harper 'the best thing to do if you are having a bad day is to end it. I am off home to bed.'

She actually went for a run instead. She ran along the river bank as it was a nice evening and road running involved stopping at junctions, crossing roads and dodging cars. She much preferred stopping for styles, avoiding any roads and dodging wildlife. She ran too far and would be sore tomorrow, but with the salad for her tea she would have a calorie deficit today and tight muscles. Something positive from the day.

Due to the run, her day and muscle ache, she had taken a bath. Speedy showers were her norm but bubbles, heat, relaxing, unwinding and the cleaning of her mind, were more important than the cleaning of her body. And that then brought her to just wrap herself in a blanket and curl on the sofa and return to the case anew.

The decision from the day was that they had been defeated. A trail had been laid to implicate an innocent. That innocent had been taken and was being held against her will. The kidnapper had worked alone and was at large, location unknown but thought to have fled abroad. The chief had made appreciative noises about "doing all that you could have" but the fact remained that they had lost. She always took that badly but it was an occupational hazard. Harper took it much more in his stride. She thought it was the years that he had spent in uniform that made the difference. His experience of talking to victims whilst stood in the defiled shell of their burgled homes (knowing that he had no means to catch the person responsible) had resigned him to not being able to fix everything. He had spent years of offering platitudes and understanding instead of convictions and justice. She had fast-tracked through the beat years and many of those were with more senior constables so her desire to always win was more robust. As a detective with resources and a good team she had a good conviction rate. She provided good direction and was strong tactically and strategically, she could solve the problems and apply well managed resources in an efficient way. She got results with good budgetary discipline. She was convincing herself that she was a good copper, despite this one.

She exhaled and ran her hands through her hair and tousled it to let the air in and some of the moisture out. She should dry it properly before bed. She covered herself with the blanket again and frowned. The job stayed in her mind though and would do for some time. All that could have been done had been done. He had been in and out quickly, one job done well and he was gone. Military planning and plenty of luck. Without the hostage taking they would have moved on a while ago but that dimension added so much. Why had he taken a hostage, he didn't seem to need one and it added elaboration into the planning. As a team they resolved that she remained alive and they left the country together.

She looked through the window at the darkening sky and hugged herself, resting her head on the back of the sofa. Perhaps she would sleep there tonight, it was still warm enough. She closed her eyes. UK ports were on the look out and should they re-enter the country on those passports then she would know. They knew some of the serial numbers on the money and that might re-enter the UK banking system at some point and their own banks, phone and credit card companies were on alert. All those were long shots.

The longest shot of all came from the friendly coastguard. She thought he was wrong on his hunch. Her own initial feeling was that Carl and Louise were in the Mediterranean, his links to France led her to that conclusion, but for someone who wanted to escape, entering into the confines of the Med as opposed to entering the vast Atlantic and then going anywhere in the world had been persuasive. So the American and friendly authorities in the West Indies were on alert. The radar and surface coverage was excellent in some areas where the US's war on drugs was underway but they were under no illusion that it was a long shot. It was a small craft in a big ocean and all they could suggest was that it was heading west, landfall unknown. With luck a smart and switched-on radar operative who was on the ball would pick up the contact, a passing surface vessel or plane would identify it as the correct type of boat and then someone locally would provide a positive ID on Carl or Louise. Alternatively they could slip into a small port unnoticed.

She reached up and turned off the light, stood and headed for the toilet and bed. She passed through the hallway and swerved around her overnight bag. It was packed and ready to go. It was a long shot but her money was on the smart and switched-on radar operative and that bag would be with her at all times for the next few months. She had not completely given up.

Forty Eight

After the passport conversation Louise had retreated to the forward cabin, closed the door and slept for a while. She continued to feel under the weather. A movement above her on the fore deck awoke her after some hours and she got up again. She washed and picked up some biscuits and water on her way above decks. Carl was still on the forward deck putting something into the chain locker. She looked at the sails, course, horizon and shipping and made some adjustments to the sails and took the boat off the auto helm and sailed for a while. He returned and silently stood before her but on the far side of the wheel. There was some distance between them but he smiled at her in a warm and loving way. She reflected that back and that made him smile more and he came around the wheel and kissed her on the forehead and then held her tightly.

'Can you forgive me?'

'Yes. It's fine. I'd rather be here than anywhere.'

He held her for a while longer and then went below and she heard him in the galley. Then at great volume music played. His choices in music were not great and usually involved guitars and volume. She was sure it would give all the whales in the Atlantic a throbbing head. He thought they might appreciate Deep Purple.

He appeared on deck after an hour clean-shaven and refreshed. They shared some broth and more tea and then swapped places at the wheel. She sat on the edge of the coving looking down the lee side. The wind had been freshening all day and they had good sailing all afternoon. The boat was heeled over and powering along well. Land would be spotted in a day or so at this pace and the boat, sea and weather seemed to be willing them to get there as soon as they could.

'You didn't eat much, are you feeling OK?' It was the first words he had said for a while and it pulled her from a day dream. She turned to look at him. He was in shorts and shirt, both were clean and had been dried in the sun and wind of that afternoon. His legs were braced against the heel of the deck and its movement and he held the wheel loosely. He had tanned well, his hair bleached and she liked those sunglasses on him. He looked at home, although thinner than she remembered, but that made his muscles (and he had a fair amount of that) appear better defined. He looked good. She had lost weight too, had tanned evenly and she was proud that those pale strap lines were a thing of the past. Her hair suffered with the salt but despite the condition of it she liked the colour. The clothes that were on board were not what she would choose for herself, that might be why she wore so little, but she would go shopping soon. She also wore shorts and one of his shirts buttoned and tied. She was confident that she also looked good. Her mind was quieter now but she still did not feel right.

'Still feeling a bit odd, but better for the food, thanks for that.'

'You're not pregnant are you?' The question was posed in jest and he let out a laugh and she breathed out suddenly.

'I hope not.' She started to think 'but I am late, what is the date today?' She went below and checked on the plotter for today's date and then tried to remember her last period. The chronology of her days at the bank had been metronomic and she always knew the date and how long it was till the weekend, till close of business, till the next holiday. Here, the days were often unremarkable and she had to push her mind back to the days at home and at the bank. She thought of her stash of tampons and pads at home in her little bathroom. She returned to the deck and a concerned looking Carl.

'You took me on the bank holiday Friday so I know that was five weeks ago and I can't remember how long before that I had my period. I know when we started to have sex; so' she waited, not wanting to say the words, 'I could be.'

'But' started Carl, 'your pills are in the forward cabin?'

'Well, there are some there but they're not mine, they're the previous owner's.'

'They are the same ones that you use, I found them in your handbag and got the same type. I got them so that you had some on board.' His voice was raised and she responded in raising her own.

'I wasn't planning to have sex with anyone, I haven't been on the pill for a while and you might remember that I was actually minding my own business before you brought me here!'

'So you weren't on the pill, but you are now though?'

She got angry. 'Yes I am now but I didn't realise that you're careful planning involved picking me up as someone to shag. Perhaps you should have pointed that out before kidnapping me.' She was getting more angry. 'I haven't been on the pill since splitting with my last boyfriend but I started soon after we started having sex and, if I am pregnant, then it must have happened in those first few days.' She calmed down, 'but I might not be, have you packed a pregnancy test?'

'No, of course I didn't' he snapped back. 'You might take the piss over my planning but it has brought us this far and made us rich. I just didn't expect you to get pregnant.'

'And are you saying I did, if you think I planned this you're fucking mad.' She spat the last line at him.

He reached over the wheel and grabbed a fist of her hair. She yelped in shock, no man had ever laid a hand on her in anger, although he seemed to be extremely calm. He lifted her slightly and she grabbed his wrist. He slowly pulled her face toward his although the ship's wheel was between them.

'Don't ever call me mad.' He said it quietly and steadily and then pulled her back to the side of the cockpit and forced her to sit down and then released her hair. He waited a few seconds.

'Of course neither of us planned this.' He looked off towards the bow, anywhere but at her. 'It's just one of those things, neither of us planned to have sex when we did. So it is not part of the plan, so we adjust the plan. When we make landfall we find a doctor and get things sorted.' He stopped with some finality.

Louise sat holding her scalp gently rubbing her hair letting his words sink in.

'You mean get an abortion; just get rid of it?'

'Yes, of course.' He seemed surprised that she was so slow on the uptake. 'A yacht is no place for a baby. We couldn't sail about with a child. With a child we would have to live on land and stay put and all this' he waved at the sails, boat and sea, 'would be for nothing. You seem to forget that we are on the run from the police, settling down to have a family now would mean us going to jail.'

'You would go to jail' she corrected.

'But they think you are involved as well, you remember that newspaper.'

'But they think that as they don't know what happened.'

Anger flashed into his eyes and his complete focus was back on her, he leaned down towards her and she flinched back.

'What does that mean, you intend to tell *them* what happened do you? Where has that thought come from? Are you going to hand me in?'

'No' she said defensively as a tear gathered in the corner of her eye 'I'm talking and thinking out loud but I could go home and have the baby, our baby. I wouldn't tell them where you were. I don't know, perhaps we could then meet up?'

'If you go home they would know where I am and find me.'

'I could wait a while before going anywhere and give you a chance to get away.'

'But hang on.' He seemed to have some revelation that he wanted to share. 'Why do you want to get away' he leaned in closer, 'I thought you wanted to be here with me, doing this, why throw all that away.' He stood up and grew to his theme. 'This is the most exciting thing that has ever happened to you, I have taken you from the dullest experience and given you all of this.' He turned a full circle with his arms outstretched, the whole horizon was hers. 'After all I have done, why would you want to give this up?'

She glowered up at him as he smiled down at her.

'You stole my life, you took everything of mine away and replaced it with your own dream. And now you'll give this all to me if I kill our child, perhaps you are used to killing, but you're stupid to think…'

She didn't get a chance to finish, he lashed out and cuffed her with some venom landing the slap high on her cheek and her ear rang. She let out a scream and fell towards the cabin wall. She lay there in surprise as tears ran. In all the experiences they had shared her fear was deepest now.

'I told you not to call me stupid. We can't sail with a baby and you can't go back to the UK; if you do that I go to prison. You have made it clear that you would be keen to tell your story and keep out of prison. You would do a deal and tell them where we have been and where I plan to go. Can't you see that the only credible thing to do is to stay together as we are now, doing what we are doing. Living the dream.' He looked down imploringly at her curled in the corner of the cockpit, one hand on her bruised face, the other on her abdomen, tears running down her face. As he smiled at her and his words faded he realised the magnitude of the contradiction. He put the auto helm on and moved towards her.

'Sorry babe, I shouldn't have hit you' he brushed her hair and took some of it from the paths of her tears. 'Think about what I said but if you do want to go back to the UK then that will be fine too.'

She flinched as he moved to kiss her on the lips and then he stood and he headed below.

He paced the saloon and shook his head as he looked towards the forward cabin. It had not gone to plan. He had laid out everything to this point and he could see his mistake. He had minutely thought through the steps and then got to the point where the two of them sailed off into the sunset. His planning had stopped then.

And now look at the consequences. He cursed himself for not thinking ahead far enough. He moved and looked down into the sink. A small puddle of crumbs and bubbles moved with the motion of the boat.

He had literally and metaphorically come so far. Too far to go back. He did love her, he thought. She had been an intrinsic part of the plan for so long and it had all worked so well, much better than he expected. He thought how long a start he would have if she went home. She could hole up in a hotel while he sailed away, but as soon as she booked a flight they would know where he had been. Could he trust her to sit on an island on her own for a few months? No. She would be pregnant, alone and abroad. He wouldn't be certain of her waiting long enough. Then he would have to talk her round to getting an abortion. It would have to be a back street one, how would that be done? He banged his head into the overhead locker with frustration as realisation grew of the correct path. The correct plan.

After all he had planned this all along. To have a boat that could be sailed single handed. He pushed back from the sink and hit out at the locker again.

Louise had heard the banging below and some cursing and now it was quiet apart from her steady crying, but she gained control and stopped that too and listened.

She had not been hit for many years and never by a man. She had not moved and still lay with her head against the cabin wall.

All was quiet but for the water on the hull and wind in the sail. Carl was calm again and she wondered what he was thinking now. She wondered if they could have a child on a boat. She was thinking of the three of them when she felt through her own temple the locker on the other side of the cabin wall being opened. The fibreglass and marine ply let go their secret as she felt the vibration of a silent hand open the locker door and reach into the back of the cupboard for something. She heard but more felt the heavy metallic object be found and be dragged from its place of rest.

Her eyes widened as she pictured what was happening just inches from her head on the other side of the bulkhead. She knew what Carl had taken from the locker. She sat up and then silently retreated onto the cabin roof. She got as far as the fairleads that led the ropes over the cabin roof and peeked down the saloon steps as Carl started up. As she was on the roof he did not see her until he had emerged but she had seen him holding the gun, low down and close into his body. She moved to retreat further and the movement caught his eye and he stood on the cockpit seat and started to reach out for her.

She panicked, swivelled and fought to get as far away as she could. She found her hand on the ropes that led over the cabin roof and she pulled up on them as she clambered toward the bow. The various sheets released from their cams and as Carl stood up to come after her the boom crashed over. The boom swept into his chest and pushed him across the cabin roof. He tumbled head first into the deck and the boom carried his momentum onto a tangle on the deck stanchions and he grasped for purchase on something before heading over the side of the boat.

There was an untidy splash as he floundered into the water and the boat sailed on under the jib sail. Louise slid from the cabin roof, rigging and sail flapping wildly about her as the boat's momentum waned. From her high vantage she soon saw him float astern, he was regaining his composure and was spitting out water and rubbing his face and eyes. He was treading water and was getting further away. Louise quickly went to the stern and put a hand on the throwing line for the life belt. As she did so she stepped over the pistol on the deck floor.

She noticed that it had landed and gouged the decking. That damage disappointed her, the deck surface was beautifully built with a lovely grain and the two of them had cared for it during this trip and now the gun lay at the end of a splintered and torn mark in its beauty. She came to her senses and looked astern as Carl drifted.

'You OK?'

'Yes; just winded.' He began a lazy swim towards her. She looked at the gun on the floor and shot a look at Carl as he headed back towards the boat. 'Can you put the ladder over?'

She thought on that. Did she want to? Moments before wasn't he coming to kill her? She pondered for a second and made a decision. A resolution.

She took the main sheet, turned it around the deck winch and hauled in so that the boat was sailing again.

'No need for that, keep the sails flapping and I will climb aboard' said a voice from close astern. The boat started to sail away.

'No don't worry about the sails. Just put the ladder…. No!'

There was frantic splashing from close under the stern as Carl realised what might be happening and he swam for his life. He had done that before on occasion. As the boat picked up speed he kept his head down and swam with desperation and energy. He felt his hand on the stern and grasped a fitting and was being dragged behind the boat. He looked up in triumph. He was close under the transom and just had to climb out. He struggled to find footing on the rudder then looked up for a handhold on deck. He looked up and saw Louise and the muzzle of the gun.

'You couldn't do it baby.' He smiled up at her then pushed out of the water and reached for the deck. There was a bright flash. A deafening bang and a silence. In that silence Carl splashed into the water. She was not sure if she had hit him or if it was the shock that had made him let go. Her eyes had been closed. She waited a few seconds then opened them and what she decided to see in the evening gloom was his right arm held aloft waving a gentle farewell.

Forty Nine

As long shots go and as stake-outs go this was not too bad. Grace stood in the intense Caribbean sun wondering about her choice of clothes. She had dispensed with her jacket and was in a glowing white blouse and an unusually short skirt. Not a normal work skirt but in this weather a girl might as well take the opportunity to get some sun.

The call had come in while she and Harper were working for the drug squad on a very dull job. It was the third such call but this looked promising enough to make the trip. Small yacht, confirmed by the US coastguard as the right make and length, approaching Cuba. They could not, or did not want to intercept and no radio response was gained. The Cuban authorities could not rouse an interest so here she was on holiday, stood at the head of the marina by the visitor's pontoon, looking out to sea. She should have binoculars, but she had not thought of that. She should have more sun cream on as well. She ruffled her hair and counted her good fortune. If she could ID them then there was the small matter of extradition but foremost in her mind was ascertaining if Louise was alive and well. She really should have brought binoculars. This was taking longer than she thought and she couldn't make out one yacht from the next. She looked at her watch and the picture of *Appeal*. It wouldn't be long now.

Fifty

Land beckoned, good food and a good shower. Louise had been able to smell it for a while now as various scents that had become unfamiliar in the month at sea were now re-introduced to the cerebellum, the gateway to the brain that filters out the routine and normal. It was now working overtime processing the things that had not been experienced for such a while.

The tide was not great at present but would be slack and turn soon. She had planned the pilotage but not called ahead. She had not talked to another person, since Carl had…well since Carl. She was not so sure that she wanted to. After he had gone she had cleaned the boat from top to bottom and then done it again after removing all of his belongings (apart from his books) placing them over the side. She had removed him from his ship and made it her own. There was resolve in what she planned to do. She would sail and travel and stop in a few months and have her baby. Then sail again. She had more money than she could have dreamt of and, now that she was on her own, a well stocked and provisioned boat. She didn't even need to make landfall, having enough water and food for another few weeks.

She looked towards Cuba, perhaps Carl had been right. She did not know what she was actually capable of. She pondered that and the thought of whether she actually wanted to go ashore and see people again. She could easily turn shoreward somewhere else. A real shower, clean sheets and air conditioning beckoned. Sail on a while longer or put into port? She involuntarily put her hand on her belly and rubbed gently and decided the direction to take.

About the Author

Kevin Dinwoodie lives and works in Cheltenham as a Business Analyst. His literary work has been published in magazines and used on radio. This is his first novel and incorporates a few of his passions; sailing, motorcycles, Cheltenham and his many friends, who are definitely *not* in this book. He has three children and his next book is intended for their reading.

Made in the USA
Charleston, SC
13 September 2016